EMILY FEATHER

and the Enchanted Door

HOLLY WEBB

EMILY FEATHER
and the Enchanted Door

■ SCHOLASTIC

First published in the UK in 2013 by Scholastic Children's Books
An imprint of Scholastic Ltd
Euston House, 24 Eversholt Street
London, NW1 1DB, UK
Registered office: Westfield Road, Southam, Warwickshire, CV47 0RA
SCHOLASTIC and associated logos are trademarks and/
or registered trademarks of Scholastic Inc.

Cover illustration © Rosie Wheeldon, 2013

ISBN 978 1 407 13092 7

A CIP catalogue record for this book is available from the British
Library.

Printed and bound by CPI Group (UK) Ltd, Croydon, CR0 4YY
Papers used by Scholastic Children's Books are made
from wood grown in sustainable forests.

7 9 10 8 6

www.scholastic.co.uk/zone

To Tom,

who read it first

1

Emily leaned over her mum's shoulder, hugging her carefully so as not to dribble the open tin of golden syrup that Emily was about to put in her flapjack mixture. "I like that one," she said thoughtfully, pointing at the fabric sample her mum was holding out, a soft strip of blue scattered with flowers and tiny birds.

"Not the red?" Her mum wafted it at her

enticingly, so that the fierce bright-orange butterflies fluttered over the fabric. The red silk glittered, only a shade brighter than her mum's hair.

Emily blinked. For a second it had looked like one of the butterflies had lifted out of the fabric and floated idly across the kitchen to the window. She wrinkled her nose and squeezed her eyelids shut for a second. It was the bright sunshine getting in her eyes. "No, I really like the blue one. It's prettier. Is it for a dress? Is this a new collection for the shop?"

"Yes, we're thinking about next summer's clothes already. I think it's going to be a skirt, this one," her mum said thoughtfully. "A maxi-skirt, with jewels scattered through the flowers.

They'll have to be hand-sewn; it'll be expensive."
She padded out of the kitchen, trailing wings of
soft, sheer fabric behind her, so that she looked
like a butterfly too.

Emily giggled. When her mum was designing
clothes, she sometimes forgot about everything
else. Even meals. But then, she did make the
most beautiful things, and not just for the shop;
she made them for Emily and her sisters too. So
it made up for having to make their own lunch,
and dinner, a lot of the time.

For Emily's last birthday, her mum had made
her a hat that looked like a cupcake, with pink
icing and little sugar flowers on it. The kind of
cake that Emily really loved making. The hat was
one of her favourite things, and she wore it loads.

It was much too hot for hats now, though. Emily leaned out of the window to breathe a bit. It was roasting in the kitchen, with the oven on. Still, it would be worth it. Flapjacks were one of her best recipes. She loved the way you just had to melt the buttery gooey mess together and stir a bit, and then it magically turned into cakey stuff when you cooked it.

"Emily!" Lark was yelling at her from down the garden. "Ems! Are you coming out? You'll melt if you stay inside all day!"

"I'm coming in a minute," Emily called back. "I just want to put these flapjacks in."

"It's too hot for cooking! You're mad! Honestly, Ems, I worry about you sometimes!" Lory joined in. "Come and sunbathe."

4

"I'm nearly done," Emily shouted out of the window. "And it won't stop you eating them, anyway, will it?"

She scooped the mixture into the tin, and then made a face at the washing up. She'd pile it into the sink and leave it till later. No one would mind. Her mum looked like she was going to be shut up in her studio for hours anyway, and her dad was in the tiny room under the stairs where he wrote his books. He wrote scary fantasy novels, and he was quite famous. He used his full name for the books, though – Ashcroft Feather, instead of just Ash, which was what most people called him. He hadn't even bothered coming out for lunch. He was stuck, he'd told everybody grumpily at breakfast, and he'd made Emily suggest ideas for really scary monsters while she was trying to eat her toast. It had slightly put her off her jam.

Emily peered out of the window at the blazing sun and decided to tie her hair back. It was too hot hanging round her neck. She wandered over to the wooden dresser that took up one wall of the kitchen. There was a mug full of hairbands and bits of ribbon on there somewhere, she was sure. It was while she was picking out a band that she found the photo, tucked under one of Lark and Lory's magazines. Emily pulled it out and stood it up on a shelf. She loved this photo. It was a rare one of all the children, sitting on the big old sofa in the living room. It had been taken when Robin was little – just turning from a baby into a boy, and losing his round, chubby face and the wispy, fair baby curls. His hair was darkening to red, and that pointed chin was starting to show. It was an odd photo, not much like other people's family portraits. Lark and Lory looked serious, and Robin was staring wide-eyed at the camera. Only Emily was smiling, in the middle of Lark and Lory, a dark-eyed, dark-haired, golden-tanned five-year-old, with Robin clutched on her lap.

The photo was in a little seashell frame, and it always lived on the dresser. But most of the time it was hard to see, because there was so much other stuff on there too. Fabric samples, and a scattering of beads. Homework. The dog's comb. Sheets of manuscript from their dad's latest novel, covered in scribble, and possibly torn into pieces. Vases of drooping flowers that Lark and Lory had brought in from the garden. But just occasionally, when it was tidy – which was usually only when her mum was lost for inspiration, and drifting around looking for something to do – the picture could be seen.

"Why does Robin look like Lark and Lory, and not like me?" Emily had asked her mum once, picking up the frame and running her fingers over the dusty shells.

Her mother had stopped on her way through to her studio, and stared at Emily for a second, her grey-blue eyes wide, before she smiled. "It just happens that way sometimes, Emily, flower. You got your looks passed on from another relative, I should think. It's just like Lory's yellow hair," she added. "No one else in the family has hair like that. We're all different."

Except that, actually, they weren't. Lory had yellow hair, it was true, but her features were just like their dad's. Her mum and dad actually looked quite alike too, Emily realized, sweeping a golden syrup drip off the side of the tin with her finger and sucking it as she went out into the garden. It was only her. She wished she knew whichever relative it was that she looked like.

Emily's house had a strange garden – it was the same size as all the other gardens on the street, but it seemed bigger somehow, and more private, because it was surrounded by trees. It was a useless sort of garden for football, or anything that needed a lawn, because there wasn't one – but it was full of tunnels, and holes, and twisted old trees, and it was perfect for playing hide-and-seek. Lark and Lory were out there somewhere, but as Emily let herself out by the back door and stood hesitating on the step, she couldn't see them at all. She could hear them, though: sharp, sweet giggling, and then a muttered comment and a riffle of pages, and another burst of laughter.

"Lark! Lory!" She set off down one of the little brick paths, calling for them. The sun was blinding, and she held her arm up across her eyes, pulling her hot hair back into the band and making for the shade under a clump of thorn trees at the edge of the garden. Where were Lark and Lory hiding?

Suddenly, Lark and Lory's voices came to her, as clear as little ringing bells, or the sharp twittering of the birds gathered above her in the thorn tree.

Emily stumbled on up the path. The sun was so bright that she was half-blinded, and she blinked as the light flickered, filtering down through the trees above her in dark bars of shadow and sunlight.

"Emily, what are you doing?" one of her sisters giggled. A thin-fingered hand caught hers and pulled her down on to a rug laid over the mossy grass. Gruff, their huge black dog, opened one eye to see who'd turned up, grunted, and went back to sleep again.

"You looked like you were about to fall over,"

11

Lark said, wrapping an arm round her shoulders and staring worriedly into her eyes. "Are you OK? You look wobbly."

"I'm fine." Emily stretched out on the rug next to her and peered at their magazine. "I guess you were right; I was melting indoors. It's much nicer out here."

"You could have brought us a drink, Ems," Lory complained.

Emily rolled her eyes but didn't say anything. Lory was so bossy sometimes. Lark was a bit more easy-going, but now that her sisters had turned thirteen, they seemed an awful lot older than they had only a few weeks ago. Too old to hang around with their little ten-year-old sister, a lot of the time.

Arguing with Lory and Lark was pointless. They always worked as a double act, and it was impossible to get the better of them. They were both staring at her now, and smiling, their heads together. The same smile, even though they weren't identical twins, and didn't, at first glance, look that much alike. Lark's streaky brown hair was nothing like Lory's golden blonde, and their eyes were different too; Lark's were much darker. But now they couldn't be anything but sisters.

Emily twirled a strand of her own dark curly hair around one finger and peered down at the magazine. The girl in the photo had dark hair like hers, with a pretty scarf tied round it. She'd like something like that.

"Are you going shopping in town later?" she

asked Lark hopefully. "Can I come too?"

Lark and Lory looked at each other thoughtfully, and then Lark said, "Maybe. . ."

"She means no," someone called from above their heads, and all three girls yelped in surprise. Lory threw the magazine at the red-haired boy leaning out of the tree above them.

"Were you spying on us?"

"Only a little bit," Robin said, laughing. He flipped round so that he was hanging off the branch by his knees, and Emily shuddered.

"Don't do that! You'll fall!"

"No, I won't. . ." Robin pushed against the tree trunk, so he was swinging. "I *never* fall," he added smugly. "Unless I want to." He swung his hands back up again, to grab one of the thinner branches, and then dangled himself down, kicking at Lory's magazine, which was stuck halfway up the trunk. "There! Got it!" It fluttered to the ground, and Robin dropped after it, landing sprawled across Lark and Lory's knees, and giggling as though it was the funniest thing he'd ever seen.

Emily stared down at him. She didn't look a bit like Robin either. He had blazing red hair like Eva, their mother, and light blue-grey eyes, and the same sharp chin and pale colouring as Lark and Lory. As he lay there giggling and wriggling away from Lark, who was tickling him, Emily could see his perfect white teeth.

She curled her knees up, wrapping her arms around them, half-watching her sisters teasing him. Then something landed in her hair, and she squealed, and Robin rolled away, hooting with laughter. "Serves you right for daydreaming!" he spluttered.

"What is it? What is it?" Emily shook her ponytail frantically, batting at it with her hands. "Did you drop a spider on me? I'm going to strangle you, Robin Feather!"

"It's only a caterpillar. . ." Lark said soothingly, picking something out of Emily's curls. She knew how much Emily hated spiders.

"No, it isn't." Robin rolled his eyes. "She's so scared of crawly things, I wouldn't even drop a caterpillar on her. It's just a catkin."

"So it is," Lark agreed. "See, Emily? Nothing to be scared of."

Emily growled, still running her fingers through her hair, just in case. But she felt better, a bit now that Robin had teased her. It was such a little brother thing to do. She was just being silly.

Of course she belonged.

Emily and her best friend Rachel wandered home from school in the sun. Emily's house wasn't far, and Rachel and her mum only lived in the next road. Now they were in Year Five, they were allowed to walk by themselves, although of course they had to bring Robin too. He was ahead of them somewhere, so he could jump out and roar. He was having that sort of a day.

Depending on how slowly they walked, they sometimes met Lark and Lory on the way back, as the secondary school was closer to home than Emily and Robin's school.

"I'm glad you're coming back to ours for a bit," Emily said happily. "It seems like we haven't hung around together properly for ages."

Rachel sighed. "I know. I can't believe I had to spend the whole weekend doing dance exams. My hair still aches, you know. It's been up in a bun for *days*."

"Awww. It's OK. We've got cake, that'll help. I made flapjacks yesterday. I warn you, though, the house is a tip. Mum and Dad were both working all weekend and no one did any tidying up. Me and Lark and Lory and Robin watched two DVDs last night, and I don't think any of us cleared up the popcorn Robin tipped all over the floor. Dad might have got rid of it, if he's finished the bit of book he was stuck on."

"You're so lucky," Rachel sighed, and Emily looked round at her in surprise. Rachel's mum and dad were divorced, and she was their only child. Rachel had a gorgeous, huge bedroom at her mum's flat, and her dad was always taking her away with him on work trips to cool places. Her mum and dad gave her pretty much anything she asked for. Just occasionally, Emily thought how nice it would be to have her parents all to herself, like Rachel did. Not all that often though. She loved her mad, loud sisters, and Robin made her laugh.

"You are! I'd love to have sisters like Lark and Lory to watch films with." Rachel leaned close and whispered, "I wouldn't even mind Robin sometimes." She laughed at Emily's disbelieving face. "At least there'd be someone else around! I just always end up watching TV on my own at home. Mum works so much."

"I suppose," Emily said doubtfully. She didn't want to agree too hard, in case she upset Rachel. She hadn't thought about it before, but even though Rachel's bedroom was gorgeous, she'd hate being mostly alone in that perfect, tidy flat. (Rachel's mum had a cleaner in twice a week, and she even tidied Rachel's room for her.) It was lovely there, but when Emily had sleepovers with Rachel, she worried about

21

making a mess — sweet wrappers looked a lot worse on Rachel's immaculate cream carpet than they did on her own creaky wooden bedroom floor. She put one arm round Rachel's shoulders. "At least you don't have big sisters teasing you all the time. And Robin pretended to drop a spider on me at the weekend. I was really cross with him."

"Uuugh. . ." Rachel shuddered. Then she said suddenly, "Is there a sort of bird called an Emily?"

Emily stared at her — it was such a weird question, totally out of the blue. "No . . . I don't think so. Why?"

"Well, because I wondered if you all had bird names. Lark and Robin are definitely birds, and I'm pretty sure Lory is too. An exotic one. A bit like a parrot. My granddad used to have one, I think."

"Oh. . ." Emily frowned. It was an odd thought. "I don't think Emily means all that much. I asked Mum once and she said it was just a Latin name."

"Huh." Rachel sighed. "That's good, though. If your name means something, you have to live up to it, don't you? Do you know what Rachel means?"

Emily shook her head. "Someone in the Bible?"

"Sheep. Honestly, I'm named after a sheep."

"It doesn't mean that," Emily sniggered.

"It does, I looked it up." Rachel shook her head disgustedly. "Actually, I don't think my mum knew that, she just called me it after my grandma, but I think she should have made an

23

effort, don't you? And don't tell anyone!"

Emily shook her head, still giggling. "I promise."

"Are you two coming?" Robin stomped up to them, looking impatient. "I can't cross the road without you, remember? I want to get home."

Emily looked at Rachel and raised her eyebrows, and Rachel shrugged.

"Mmm. OK. Maybe I'm only jealous of your sisters."

After the things she and Rachel had talked about on the way home, Emily looked carefully at her house as they went through the front gate. She didn't usually; it was just her house, the house on the corner. Messy, a little bit shabby, and surrounded by garden. She was used to it.

The front gate creaked as they pushed it open, she noticed. Did it always? It was a nice noise, sort of friendly. The front garden was tiny, more like a bit of the big back garden that had squeezed round to the front to cover up the wheelie bins. The house itself was tall and thin – even taller because of the odd little turret that jutted out of the attic in one corner, like someone had borrowed a bit of a castle and randomly stuck it on to an oldish but otherwise normal-looking house.

Everyone always assumed that the attic was Emily's dad's writing room, because of the turret – the little pointy witch's hat of a tower looked exactly right for her dad's sort of books.

They were all about warriors and dragons and orcs and that sort of thing. But actually, it was Emily's room, and there was a window seat running round the inside of the turret that Emily kept all her bears on. Which wasn't quite so dramatic.

The green front door had a brass mermaid door knocker that sent a hollow thumping through the house when anyone banged it. The mermaid generally looked bad-tempered, Emily thought, but then people hit her against the door all the time, so it was only to be expected.

The stained-glass panels sent jewel-coloured streaks up and down the walls of the hallway as Robin flung the door open. He was gone, dropping his bag and kicking off his shoes before he made for the kitchen. Emily and Rachel followed him.

"Are there any of those flapjacks you made yesterday left?" Robin asked hopefully, looking round the kitchen and sniffing like a questing hound.

Emily pulled the tin out of one of the cupboards and handed it to him. "Leave some for us," she said quickly, as he started to pile flapjacks on to one hand.

"All right! They're only little," Robin protested. "I'm really hungry. School lunch was pasta with glue, again. I just ate the garlic bread."

There were so few flapjacks left after he'd raided them that Emily and Rachel decided it was simpler just to take the rest of the tin upstairs, with a couple of bananas to go with them.

The stairs were probably the main difference from Rachel's flat, Emily thought to herself as they went up to her room. She couldn't imagine living all on one floor. Stairs were nice. They were good for sulking on when Robin was being a pain, and they were a very useful place to leave things that you needed to put away and just hadn't quite got round to taking up to your room yet. Plus they were a good place for all the random paintings and odd old mirrors that her parents had collected over the years.

A lot of the paintings were ancient ones that Mum said had come from her parents' house. They were so dark, Emily could hardly see what was in most of them – just a shadowy figure here and there, or a pale, ghostly face shining out of the dirt and thick, treacly varnish. There were framed school photos dotted in and out of them, and pictures that Lark and Lory and Emily and Robin had drawn over the years, but most of the paintings and mirrors had heavy wooden frames, carved with curls and scrolls, that were far more interesting than the murky images they held.

Emily's favourite was an enormous mirror that stood on the landing at the top of the stairs, just before the little, rickety flight that led up to her room, which had been the attic once.

The mirror was on the wall between Lark's room and Lory's, and it looked ancient. It had a gold frame, like a garland of flowers twirled around the glass, and so carefully carved that you could see the stalks of all the flowers, and catch glimpses of tiny birds and mice lurking behind them. Little touches of faded paint brightened the petals and the birds' feathers, and Emily loved it. It was a flattering mirror, too. Something about the light pouring in from the big window on the landing made the reflections glow with a softness that was like candlelight – like the light that the mirror had been made for. There were still candle holders nestled in the woodwork of the frame, with old stubs of candles in them. They made Emily feel that she ought to have her hair arranged in bunches of ringlets and wear long dresses with frilly petticoats.

Emily peered into the mirror as she and Rachel went past, scrunching up her wavy hair into a sort of topknot and expecting to see a Victorian version of herself staring back at her. Instead, she only saw herself, pink from sitting in the sun at lunchtime, her ponytail gone crooked. Emily made a face at herself as she tried to pull her ponytail straight.

Emily glanced round at Lark's door, and Lory's on the other side of the mirror. They reminded her that she and Rachel had better hurry up. Her sisters would be back soon, and they would be after a sugar boost too. Lark's door looked a soft sage green today – it was a trick of the light on the landing; both her sisters' rooms had doors that seemed to change colour. Lark's could be anything from bright emerald to grey, and Lory's went from creamy yellow to scarlet depending on which way you looked at it, and how hot a day it was. Today it was a burning sunset orange.

Robin's door was always the same sky blue, but it moved. It didn't really, of course; Emily knew that. It just seemed to, because of the shadows. She'd seen his door in between Lark's room and Lory's once, and her favourite mirror had been inside his room, hanging over his bed. That had been in the middle of the night, though, when she'd come down to go to the loo, so she'd probably been dreaming.

But it was that sort of house. Emily was used to it, but it did surprise people sometimes. Rachel was standing on the landing looking confused right now.

Emily pushed her gently in the direction of

the little flight of stairs that led up to her attic bedroom. "Come on, I'm starving. . ."

Rachel blinked at her gratefully, and they hurried up the stairs together. Emily could hear thumping steps behind them, and she glanced back down to see Gruff following her, his huge grey wiry muzzle twitching hopefully. "Oh, all right. You can have a bit. But just a little bit. I'm hungry too, and I made them!"

Emily's door never seemed to change colour. It was purple, and it was always exactly where she wanted it to be. She adored her bedroom. She knew that when she was little, she'd had a tiny little bedroom that opened off her parents' room, on the floor below Lark and Lory. But somehow she couldn't remember sleeping anywhere else.

33

It wasn't a massive bedroom – but it was Emily's, and no one else's. In a big family (especially a big family with two bossy older sisters and a little brother who could charm the birds out of the trees if he could be bothered to make the effort), that was something special. Her bed was tucked into the corner behind the door, and then there was room for a chest of drawers and not a lot else in the main part of the room – but there was the turret too. It bulged out of the end of the room, round, and not all that big. Dusty beams held up the pointy roof part, and Emily hung things off them sometimes – little strings of bells, and sparkly baubles and snowflakes at Christmas.

It was the windows that made it special, though. The glass in them was wavy – there

34

was no other way to describe it. It was old, old glass, her dad had told her. Probably the original glass from when the house was built, nearly two hundred years before. It was greenish, and thick, and it rattled in the wind and let the cold draughts in, but Emily didn't mind. When she sat at her table in the turret and stared out of those windows, the glass made it look as though she was gazing at forests, and palaces with turrets like hers – not the houses on the other side of the street. Emily sat on the cushioned bench around the windows watching, and dreamed, or sometimes she drew, stretching pieces of paper out across her table and trying to catch the shadowy fairy-tale places that she saw sideways through the glass. Her dad had

35

framed one of the drawings, and he kept it on the wall in his tiny study. Emily's mum said she was too imaginative, which Emily thought was very unfair, because obviously Emily's drawing had come from her; she drew all the time. But she'd only said it after Emily's teacher had sent home a note about unsatisfactory homework. Her mum and dad had been quite upset. They weren't used to notes from school. Lark and Lory and Robin were all brilliantly clever. Emily wasn't stupid, but she was a lot better at cooking and drawing than she was at things like maths.

Now if the homework was something that really needed concentrating on, Emily did it on the other side of the table, sitting on the bench seat and looking away from the windows. It didn't work very well, though. She could still see the glass out of the corners of her eyes, and she could feel the stories going on behind her.

She and Rachel curled up on the window seat and nibbled flapjacks, with Gruff sitting on the floor between them, his huge head resting on the cushions so he could stare up at them with melty, loving eyes. It was impossible not to feed him when he looked like that, and he made it very clear that he wanted flapjack; he was not being fobbed off with banana. Banana was not for dogs.

"I wonder why he doesn't get fat," Rachel said thoughtfully. "*Everyone* feeds him. Even people in the street. Remember that little girl giving him her ice cream?"

37

Emily shuddered. "Of course I do. Her mum yelled at me for ages. She wouldn't believe me when I said he hadn't snatched it, and Gruff just stood there licking it off his whiskers and looking blissed out. It was awful."

Gruff sniffed thoughtfully at the cushions in case he'd missed any crumbs, sighed heavily, and stalked away, clicking and thudding down the wooden stairs.

Emily leaned back against the windows, her cheek against the cool glass, and watched the thin, hazy clouds floating past, twisting themselves into fantastical shapes. She wondered if Rachel could see them, or if it was just her. Maybe there was something strange about her. No one else in her family seemed to see odd things out of the corners of their eyes. When she'd told Robin about the doors changing colour he'd looked at her as if she was mad, and then snorted with laughter.

Still, Emily didn't mind. She didn't even mind that much that they were all cleverer than she was, though it did make school reports at the end of the year a bit depressing. She wouldn't give up being dreamy and seeing things for being good at spelling.

"Rachel! Your dad called! He's on his way round to pick you up." Eva was shouting from the kitchen, and the girls sighed, and stretched, and clattered back down the stairs.

Emily only glanced into the mirror on the landing to see if her nose was still red – it felt as though she might have burned a bit in the sun, and she was hoping it wasn't going to peel. She looked at herself anxiously – but she wasn't there. The mirror was full of mist.

Emily blinked at it, wondering what had happened. Had her mum tried to clean the glass? It had always been mottled, spotted with dark patches, where the old glass was losing its silver, but it had never been greyish before. It hadn't looked like this on her way *up* the stairs, either.

She took a step closer, looking into the misty surface, and lifted a hand to run her fingertips over the glass. Maybe it was just damp? The mirror wasn't that far from the bathroom, and Lark and Lory both took ages in the shower, and left the bathroom all steamed up. But then

Emily stopped, her fingers still reaching out to touch the glass, and she stared. She blinked in confusion, and looked back again.

In the mirror, gazing out at her, was a face.

Not hers.

Not even the oddly lit version of her own face that Emily had imagined she might see. This was someone completely different. The skin was pale – even paler than Lory and Lark – and the hair was a greenish-gold, swirling around the girl's head with a thick flatness, like water weed floating in a river. Her eyes were a shallow, silvery green, glittering even in the dim light of the mirror-place. They were wild, exciting eyes, and the creature in the mirror was laughing, Emily was sure. Her lips were drawn back over pretty, pointed little teeth, and Emily could see a glimpse of the bright pink of her sharp tongue.

Emily lifted her hand again, wondering if her fingers would go through the mirror if she tried to touch the glass. Maybe it wasn't glass at all any more. It looked almost like water. She brought her fingers closer, not quite daring to touch. What if the girl in the mirror caught Emily's hand, and pulled her in? Or what if she *didn't*? Wouldn't that be almost worse?

"Who are you?" Emily whispered, running her fingertips over the flowers on the mirror frame and gasping as her fingers tingled, and a twining of white wild roses and dark ivy appeared around the girl in the mirror. Her greenish hair seemed to flush golden, like wheat stalks, and she smiled

42

more widely, and the white rosebuds opened around her. Emily could smell them, a very faint, sweet, spicy scent that wafted out around the landing.

Where was she, this strange girl? Was there somewhere else behind the mirror? It was only Lory's wardrobe behind that wall, Emily was quite sure. Unless – unless it was a *different* sort of place. The mirror felt so inviting, almost like a door. A door that was just a little open. Emily felt a small spark of excitement deep in the middle of her. Had she opened it? Had *she* made the mirror change?

She moved her fingers closer to the glass, wondering what it would feel like, and the girl in the mirror watched her eagerly, raising her own

43

fingers, as though she wanted to touch them to Emily's through the glass.

She looks like Lory, Emily thought dreamily, as her skin brushed the chill surface of the mirror. She blinked a little, and stared more closely, sharply at the girl. *Was* it Lory? Was this all some kind of a trick? Mum would kill Lory if she'd made a hole out of the back of her wardrobe.

But the eyes were different, Emily decided. Lory had golden-yellow eyes, with brown flecks in them, and this girl's eyes were silvery-green. Besides, how would Lory fill her wardrobe with mist, and pale roses? It wasn't Lory's wardrobe she was staring into, it was somewhere else. Another place. And Emily wanted to go there too.

44

She pressed her fingers to the glass, feeling that eerie tingling again, and the girl in the mirror smiled at her. Her own white fingers stretched out to Emily's, and Emily gasped as the icy glass seemed to soften and give under her fingertips. It rippled, and bubbled, and Emily felt something shiver through her, right the way to the ends of her hair.

Then it all stopped. The glass hardened and cleared, and there was only her own face staring back at her – white and frightened, but somehow excited too. And behind her in the mirror was Rachel, frowning with worry, her brownish hair and freckled nose looking strangely normal after that eerie girl.

Rachel was holding her arm, Emily realized.

Her friend must have come back upstairs to see why she'd stopped, and grabbed her. Just as – just as something was about to happen. Emily wasn't sure whether to be grateful or not.

"Are you all right? You look really funny." Rachel took hold of Emily's other arm, as though she was worried Emily might fall down. "Is that why you were looking in the mirror? You've gone ever so pale." She moved a smidge backwards, but kept hold of Emily. "Are you going to be sick?"

"No . . . I don't think so." Emily closed her eyes for a second. There were odd sparkles and flashes at the back of them, like white flowers. What had happened? There had been a girl. . . She could hardly remember. It was as if the mist in the mirror had swirled through her head too – everything was vague, and all the shapes seemed wrong.

Emily shook her head firmly, and shivered as all the glittering lights swayed and whirled behind her eyes. "No. I'm OK." She took a shaky step away from the mirror, and it seemed suddenly easier to breathe. She looked back at it – pretty as ever, the carvings delicate, the paint faded. There was nothing to show what had just happened.

Perhaps it hadn't happened at all. Maybe Rachel was right.

Something cold nudged her hand, and Emily jumped.

"It's only Gruff," Rachel told her gently.

"Oh. . ." Emily patted the enormous dog on his grey head. "Hey, Gruff."

"He just turned up, I didn't even hear him coming," Rachel murmured. "Oh, there's my dad!" she added, as someone banged the mermaid door knocker. "Are you OK, Ems? I've got to go, you know what Dad's like if you make him hang around."

Emily nodded. "I'm fine, honestly." She managed a grin. "Got up too fast, that's all. I just need another flapjack!" She hurried down the stairs with Rachel and said goodbye looking almost normal. But when the door shut, her legs wobbled again, and she shivered.

Gruff let out a low, grumpy sort of growl, and pushed at her. He was so big, he fitted snugly just under her elbow. He squidged himself close and nudged Emily till she sat down on the bottom step of the stairs. Then he gazed at her suspiciously, as though he thought she might be about to keel over. He was squashing her feet, his heavy greyish head resting solemnly in her lap. She couldn't move, pressed into the stairs by the weight of dog, as though he was guarding her.

Emily looked down at Gruff, his shining eyes as black as liquorice. Did he know what had happened? Had she imagined it all? "I wish you could tell me," she murmured, under her breath, but Gruff just let out a steamy huff of breath and rubbed his muzzle against her leg. If he knew what had happened, he wasn't saying.

3

That night, Emily lay in bed with Gruff stretched out just below her feet. He didn't always sleep in her room, only sometimes, but he'd been following her around all day. He'd even sat on her feet during dinner. Luckily, with Lark and Lory complaining about a new teacher, the meal was noisy enough that no one really noticed how pale and quiet Emily was. Her mum did ask if she was all right, but Emily only said she was sleepy from the heat. It might even be true – maybe it was just the hot sun that was making her see weird things. But her bedroom windows were full of pictures even in the winter.

Perhaps there was something weird about *her*? Emily shifted carefully, trying not to dislodge Gruff from her feet and burying her face into her pillow. Maybe she could see things that other people couldn't? She scrunched her eyes more tightly closed. She wasn't sure if she wanted to see anything strange. Especially not now, in the dark.

Maybe you're a witch, she thought to herself as she sank into sleep.

Emily shifted, and sighed, and turned over, and Gruff huffed and wriggled and curled up further down the bed.

She began to dream, strange glimpses of a lush, leafy riverbank, overhung with willow trees. She was sitting in the shadows, not the full sun, watching the water as it flowed by. The river looked deep and dark along the central channel, but the banks sloped gently down, and the water glittered silvery as it rippled over the stones close to her feet. It looked like the mirror, she remembered vaguely, though which mirror, and why it was important, she didn't know.

She crawled a little way forward, to see the water better, and lay down with her chin propped in her hands, to gaze into the shallows. Weeds were streaming in the gentle current, rippling like green silken ribbons, and she dipped her fingers in the water to stroke them.

Then she smiled delightedly as a tiny little see-through silvery fish darted past her fingers, followed by another, and another.

She was so absorbed watching the fish that she didn't look up at first, when the girl came. Emily realized gradually that someone was sitting next to her, dipping their toes in the clear water and humming a little.

Emily looked round at her, trying to sit up, and gasped as the silken ribbon-weed bound itself tightly around her fingers, pulling her closer to the water.

The girl next to her clicked her tongue in

53

irritation – whether at her or the weed, Emily wasn't sure – and flung a handful of sandy mud into the clear water. The weed let go of Emily with a reluctant sucking sensation, and she pulled her hand away.

"Thank you," she whispered to the girl. "I must have got twisted up in them somehow. . ." Her voice trailed away. She hadn't got tangled up. The weeds had tried to hold on to her. And she knew the girl who was staring at her now. She had seen her before somewhere – that hair that was greenish-gold, like the water weed. The pointed ears and silvery eyes. But with the wispy, infuriating logic of dreams, Emily couldn't remember where. She stared down at the water again, frowning and trying to think. The girl

54

was still dabbling her toes in the shallows, and Emily gazed at them, suddenly realizing that they were webbed. Greenish fans of skin spread out between each of her long toes. Emily looked at the girl's fingers, which were the same, and swallowed. Whoever she was, and wherever Emily had seen her before, she wasn't human.

The girl smiled at Emily, but when she spoke, her voice was very serious. "Don't touch things you don't understand," she whispered in Emily's ear, her voice hissing and soft. Then she slipped down the little bank and stood ankle-deep in the river, staring back at Emily. She flicked her water-weed hair and dived smoothly into the deeper part of the river, her silvery dress sliding into the water as though it was made of water itself.

Emily saw her swimming away – nothing like the splashy, energetic sort of swimming she had been taught when they had lessons at school, but a slow, strong weaving of her body, like a seal. The girl glanced round one more time, and then she was gone, into the depths of the river.

Emily stared after her, and then something was scratching at her foot. When she looked down at it, she was wrapped up in her thin quilt, and Gruff was stretched over her feet again, staring at her with huge black eyes.

Emily woke up still tired, her eyes gritty and sore. It was an effort to drag herself out of bed and go downstairs for breakfast. She could only half remember her dream, but it must have been a very vivid one, to have left her feeling so worn out. Gruff followed her out of the room. Emily ran her fingers over the great dog's rough fur, wondering why Gruff was still sticking so close to her. Was it something to do with the mirror, and the dream? Could he tell how strange she was feeling? He was very good at looking after people – he had hauled her out of the garden pond once, when she was tiny. She couldn't remember him ever being as watchful as this though – usually he spent most of his time with Robin, although he liked to curl up on Ash's feet while he was working.

"Emily, are you planning to brush your hair this morning, or are you going to school with a bird's nest on your head?" Lark asked, twirling a strand of Emily's knotted dark hair around her finger.

"Don't. . ." Emily muttered crossly. "I'll brush it after breakfast, I'm too tired now. I had weird dreams all night, and I feel like I didn't sleep at all."

Eva looked up from the piece of toast she was eating with one hand, while she scribbled in a sketchbook with the other, and asked lightly, "What sort of dreams, Emily love?"

Emily flumped down into a chair, and Gruff nosed closer to Eva's knee, where he could sit and beg for toast.

"I can't remember them all." Emily sighed. "They were really odd. I kept going to places, strange places, and I met a girl. A girl with webbed feet. And the funny thing was," she added slowly, realizing it herself for the first time, "it's really strange, but I think I'd seen her before. When I wasn't asleep. I saw her –" she glanced around the table, to make sure that no one was going to laugh, but her family were all staring at her, their faces blank "– I saw her in the mirror on the landing," she finished, in a hurried mutter.

"In the mirror?" her father asked sharply, nearly upsetting the huge mug of tea that was in front of him. Gruff leaned over the edge of the table and licked up the wave of tea that had slopped over the side.

"What, that big old flowery one?" Lory asked curiously.

"Mmm." Emily nodded, ducking her head so

she didn't have to see them laughing. But no one did. "It must have been a mistake. . ." she faltered. She had expected them all to tell her she was being silly, or that she was making it up. When no one seemed to think it was funny in the slightest, it all seemed a lot more real.

Eva reached out and stroked Emily's rough hair, gently teasing out the tangles. "Was that yesterday, Emily? Was that why you were so quiet at dinner? Rachel said something about you feeling sick. It's this heat, isn't it? I'm sure that's what it was. And that landing is very dark, with the stairs, and that small window. . ."

It wasn't, but no one said so. Even Robin nodded solemnly, and Emily gazed around at them all, suddenly wondering if they thought she was a bit stupid. The ditzy one. . .

"Anyway, it's time for school. You need to get your stuff or you're going to be late," Eva said, standing up and sweeping all the cereal bowls off to the sink, even though Robin had his spoon halfway to his mouth. For once, he didn't argue, just took the spoon over to add it to the pile, and went out into the hallway to get his shoes.

Emily stared after him, gaping, and Eva flapped her hands at her. "Go on, Emily! Rachel's going to be here any minute!"

Emily swallowed. "But, Mum. . ."

"Not now, Emily. Really. Not now."

And her mum sounded so serious that Emily just went to get ready for school.

61

"I don't think I want to go out, it's so hot. . ."
Emily murmured, hesitating at the door to the
playground at break. "I'm going to go to the
library."

Rachel nodded. "I know what you mean. I
don't mind. It'll be nice and cool in there."

They wandered off along the corridor to the
library, and Rachel curled up on one of the
beanbags with a book, but Emily couldn't settle.
She kept picking books up and putting them
back again. Nothing sounded interesting. Not as
interesting as her odd dreams, and the strange
way her family were behaving, anyway.

She ran her fingers along the spines of the
books, hoping she could find one to take her
mind off things. The plastic book covers felt

sticky in the heat, and the titles swam in front of her eyes.

But then Emily's fingers ran across a bumpy, frayed old book that felt pleasantly cool. The leather binding had gilt letters pressed into it, but they were so faded she had to take the book off the shelf to read them. It was heavy, even though it was quite a small book, and as she picked it up the cool leather seemed to warm and glow in her hands, as though the dusty maroon had turned blood red.

Grimm's Fairy Tales, Emily read, peering at the letters. She wrinkled her nose thoughtfully. It didn't look like any book of fairy tales she'd read – shouldn't it be pink, and a bit sparkly? And *Grimm*? She giggled to herself. Not the best name for somebody who was going to write about fairies and unicorns and stuff. Still, she wanted to read the book – really, really wanted to, actually, which was weird when a couple of minutes before, all the books had looked boring.

Emily took the book over to the beanbag next to Rachel and huddled up in a patch of sunlight. The sun made the gilt letters on the front cover glitter, and Emily drew in a hungry breath, fumbling at the cover to open up the book. She blinked as the pages fell open, surprised at how small the type was, and how black against the yellowy cream of the fragile paper. Words and enchanting phrases sprang out at her here and there, and Emily frowned, forcing herself to start at the beginning of the story.

It was "Cinderella", she realized with a little smile. It had always been one of her favourite stories, and she loved the Disney film, with all those silly singing mice. But this wasn't the version of the story she knew, she discovered as she kept reading. She'd never known that after Cinderella's mother died she'd haunted a tree. . . And there was no fairy godmother in this version; the mother's tree shook its leaves and ball dresses floated down. Emily read on to the end of the story, fascinated. There was a little illustration close to the end, a picture of the prince on his horse, with a girl behind him, but her foot was dripping blood. Uuurgh! Cinderella's sisters had cut bits of their feet off to try and fit into the slipper! That definitely wasn't in the film. . . It was the strangest version of the story she had ever read.

The one that came after was "Snow White", and Emily eyed the illustrations cautiously. Even in the versions she'd read, it was a bit gory. The wicked queen made the huntsman bring back Snow White's heart. It couldn't get much more horrible, surely?

Apparently, it could. The queen actually ate it – it wasn't really Snow White's heart, of course, but still. Yuck. No illustration of that bit, though, luckily. . .

Curious, Emily turned over the page to find the next story. The title was drawn in a garland of flowers, very pretty ones that reminded Emily of the mirror on the landing at home. She ran her finger over the letters and shivered. "The Changeling Child". She had never heard of this story – it wasn't in any book of fairy tales she'd ever seen before.

Once upon a time, a woman longed to have a child. Then after many years of waiting, her baby was born. The mother loved the little girl so much that she told everyone she met how perfect her baby was, how beautiful, how well-behaved, how clever. Even though her husband warned her not to make so much of their daughter, in case it should be unlucky, she couldn't stop herself.

Until one morning, when the mother woke, and looked into the baby's cradle, her perfect child had gone. Left behind in its place was a strange baby that seemed to have been carved out of wood, with ugly staring eyes, and a mouth full of sharp little wooden teeth.

Emily caught her breath, staring at the illustration. The wooden baby looked like some sort of horrible doll, but even in the picture, she could see that it was alive.

What had happened to the real baby? That was what Emily really wanted to know, but the story seemed to be all about the family that was left behind. Emily skimmed through the next few lines. The mother walked into the deep woods to find an old woman who might be a witch, to ask her how to get the baby back. But the witch's remedy cost the mother all the money she had saved up, and even then all it did was cause the wooden baby to fly up the chimney and disappear, back to the underground world of the fairies.

The real baby never came back. The witch told the mother that she had loved the little girl too much, and that the fairies who had taken her would never give her up.

When the mother had a second child, she dressed him in ragged clothes, and smudged ash on to his bright hair, so that this time the fairies wouldn't steal her darling away.

And as for the little girl – Emily's heart beat suddenly faster – she was still in the land under the hill, never growing older, never going home.

Emily slammed the book shut, gasping. She had been so sure that the little girl would be saved in the end – it was a fairy story, after all! Even though the story said she never grew up, the face of the child in the illustration at the bottom of the page *was* old. Old, and terribly sad, although she was only two or three, in an old-fashioned long dress and a little cap. There were long-eared fairy faces drawn around her, and fairy fingers stroked her arms. She had stared out of the page at Emily, as though she could see her watching.

Emily shook her head. That was stupid. It was a printed book, that was all. How could the little girl have been looking at her? She brushed her fingers over the pages, trying to decide whether or not to open the book again. She had the strangest feeling that the little changeling girl wanted her to . . . that she felt Emily understood her story.

The bell shrilled for the end of break, and Emily jumped so suddenly that she almost dropped the book.

"Come on, Emily." Rachel had already slipped her library book back on to the shelf, and she was holding out her hand to pull Emily up.

Emily hesitated. They weren't supposed to take books out of the library when there wasn't a teacher there to scan them. But this book felt special, almost as though it had been put in the library just for Emily. She wanted to take it home, so much. She couldn't just put it back on the shelf. What if someone else took it out? She pulled the book close to her, cradling it fiercely. She needed it!

"Emily, come on!" Rachel was giving her a

weird look, and Emily swallowed and forced a smile, and took Rachel's hand to let her friend pull her off the beanbag.

She would come back at lunch, and get the book out of the library then to take home. She wanted to read all of it. There might even be another story about the changeling child. One where she got back home.

For now Emily waited until Rachel turned round, and quickly shoved the book underneath the beanbag. No one would find it there.

Emily sped back to the library at lunchtime, eager to find the book again. The room was dark after the corridor, where the sun was pouring through the big windows, and it was completely empty.

Emily hurried over to the beanbag. She ferreted under it for the book, her breathing tight until she found it, the leather cool and silky under her fingers. She pulled it out and it fell open at the same page, the changeling girl staring out at her again.

Emily drew in a sharp breath, sure that the little girl was about to ask her something, to tell her secret. It was the oddest feeling. Emily loved books, and she sometimes liked to imagine herself into them, but this was different. Now she felt as though the book knew she was there. The changeling girl wanted to talk to her, Emily was almost sure.

"What are you looking at? What book's that?"

Emily tried to close it, but Robin grabbed it

first, snatching the book out of her hands and staring at her furiously.

"It's just a library book. . ." she stammered. "An old fairy-tale book. Give it back, Robin!" How had he even got here? She hadn't seen him come in, or heard him, even in the silent library. He was just there.

"You can't have this." Robin didn't sound like her little brother, Emily thought. It was as though someone much older was talking from inside him. He was angry. Not cross, in a you-ate-the-last-biscuit kind of way. Deeply, really angry. And scared.

"I don't understand. . ." Emily started to say, and then Robin wasn't there any more. Or rather, Emily wasn't. Now she was outside on the grass with all the others, and there was a half-made daisy chain in her hands.

But I wasn't here! I was in the library! Emily thought, staring down at her fingers, which were threading daisies all by themselves. *I was!*

But at the same time, she felt as if she had been outside since the beginning of the lunch. Making the daisy chains was really annoying; all the daisies had those skinny stems that it was hard to make the holes in. It had taken ages to make a big enough chain for a necklace.

Then a shadow fell over her daisy chain, and she looked up to see Rachel leaning over her. Emily smiled up at her gratefully. Rachel would know she hadn't been outside. Emily opened her mouth to ask what was going on, but Rachel spoke first.

"I thought you were asleep there for a minute!" Rachel yawned, and lay down on the grass next to her. "Actually, I feel quite sleepy too. Nice daisy chain. Can you make one for me?"

4

Emily felt like she was sleepwalking through the rest of the day. She watched herself working on a history project with Rachel and the others, and was amazed at how normal she sounded. It must have been another dream. Rachel had said that Emily looked sleepy. She'd had lunch, then fallen asleep making daisy chains, and dreamed the way the girl in the book had been waiting for her. But it wasn't just any dream, was it? It had meant something.

There had been so much weird stuff happening, Emily thought to herself, as she tried to draw a Roman chariot to go on to their wall display. She was the only one who could draw horses, Rachel said, so she had to do it. It was a good thing – the other three were arguing about where to put stuff, and Emily could draw and think at the same time.

First the odd girl in the mirror. Then she'd turned up again in Emily's dream, by the river. And there were other dreams, she was sure; she just couldn't quite remember them. And now the girl in the book.

If she'd brought someone in a book to life,

maybe she had some sort of power? Emily wondered, as she rubbed out one of the horse's legs, which wouldn't go properly the way it was supposed to. She smiled to herself. The power to talk to – well, what was that greenish girl? Emily sort of wanted to say she was a fairy, but fairies sounded like pretty, glittery things with wings. There hadn't been any glitter. At all.

Did it mean she would be able to do magical stuff herself? That might be exciting – once she'd got used to it. She was a good cook – brilliant, Mum said. Maybe there was something extra in her cooking! She'd been mixing up spells and cake. . . Emily smiled to herself and stretched out her fingers, letting her pencil roll on to the table. Nothing looked any different. Her hands

79

weren't glowing; her fingers didn't look like they were going to shoot sparks out of the ends or anything. The pencil didn't hover in the air. She didn't *feel* magical. She just felt confused. And desperate to talk to Robin. He'd been in her dream, after all. Maybe he'd felt something too?

In fact, she was going to have a serious talk with him on the way home. Rachel was staying at school for netball, so Emily could ask him if he knew what was going on. And if he did know, how he'd . . . done whatever it was he did. And why! She'd been in the library, she knew she had, and then somehow Robin had made her move.

As soon as the bell went for the end of school, Emily hurried to grab all her stuff and get out to the gate, which was usually where they met

Robin to walk home.

He was there already, waiting for her, but there were too many people around to ask him what had happened. Emily didn't want anyone listening. So she had to settle for staring at Robin meaningfully, with a "we need to talk" look.

Robin opened his eyes very wide, so that the sun shone on them and they looked pale and silvery and flat.

Emily gritted her teeth. She knew that look. It was the one Robin always used when he was trying to avoid doing something. He had an amazing ability to slide out of things – small spaces, arguments, jobs he didn't fancy doing. He would be there one minute, and the next he would have disappeared, so quickly and cleanly that people usually forgot he'd been there at all.

She grabbed his hand and pulled him out of the school gate, hurrying him down the road, far enough in front of the other parents and children to talk without being heard.

"Robin, what happened at lunchtime?" Emily asked urgently.

"What?" Robin frowned, gazing back at her indignantly. He looked so surprised that Emily believed him for a second. Only a second, though.

"Don't pretend!" she begged. "I thought it was a dream, but you were there, weren't you? I can tell! You do know what I'm talking about!" There were a few people up the other end of the road, and she pushed Robin into the edge of someone's garden path, hidden by bushes, and shook him by the arm. "Please, Robin, I want to know! Stop pretending! You made me move out of the library, and you almost made me forget I was even there. . ." Her voice trailed away. It sounded so stupid. So unlikely. Robin was her little brother. He was only eight. But she hadn't imagined it; she couldn't have dreamed up anything that weird.

Robin wriggled out of her grip and stood on the pavement glaring at her, red patches showing on his pale cheeks for once. "I'm telling Mum you did that! You're not allowed to grab me. Lark! Emily's being mean!"

Her sisters must have walked very fast from their school, Emily thought, looking round at

83

them in surprise. Perhaps they'd got out early. All three of them were staring at her now.

"What did you do to him?" Lory sighed. "Can't you two just leave each other alone for once?"

"But I'm not being mean. . ." Emily frowned. She was sure something had happened at lunchtime, but it was so hard to remember when they were all staring at her. "There was a book, and a little girl. Robin was there, I know he was. . . I can't think. . . I have to go home." Emily took off down the road, knowing that they were all staring after her, and not caring.

Emily could hear her mum and Lark and Lory at the bottom of the stairs, talking about her. She couldn't hear what they were actually saying, just buzzing voices, and her own name here and there. They were probably telling her mum there was something wrong with her. Her head ached, and her eyes were sticky and sore from crying.

Emily rolled over, trying to find a cool place on her pillow. What was wrong with her? She almost hoped she was ill. It would explain the strange dreams, and the faces in mirrors. Maybe the book was just a book and she had flu, and she'd just imagined the pictures moving.

She wasn't quite sure that flu explained what Robin had done, though... But people did black out sometimes when they were ill? Maybe that was what she'd done? Emily blinked up at the ceiling. Perhaps she was *really* ill? Life-threateningly ill?

"Mum. . ." she called anxiously, and there was a listening sort of silence from the bottom of the stairs.

"Are you OK, Emily?" her mum called, very quietly.

"No. . ."

Her mum hurried up the stairs and crouched down by the side of Emily's bed. "Lark and Lory said you were upset, but they thought you wanted to get over it on your own. What's happened, sweetheart?"

"I don't know. . ." Emily's voice shook. "I keep having really strange dreams. I was in the library at school, or I thought I was. There was this book – and then Robin made me move. I was in the library and then all of a sudden

I was outside. Or I think I was. But that isn't possible. I think I've got flu and it's making me see things." She looked hopefully at her mum. She wanted to be offered herbal tea, and hot water bottles, and duvets on the sofa. And most of all, to be told that it was all OK.

"You're getting to that age," her mum said, very quietly.

"What age?" Emily stared at her. What was so special about being ten?

Unless it was to do with that *growing up* talk that all the Year Five girls had been shepherded off to the library for at the beginning of the year. About your body changing. But no one had mentioned anything about dreams. Or mirrors suddenly having people in the back of them.

Emily had gone straight home and asked Lark and Lory what it was all about. She felt sorry for people who didn't have older sisters to ask.

"Do you mean hormones?" she asked Mum, feeling quite pleased with herself for remembering what they were called.

But her mother stared at her blankly. "No . . . oh, well, that isn't what I meant. But that's probably it." She smiled, but only her mouth moved. Her eyes still looked worried. And almost sad, Emily thought, feeling more mixed up than ever.

"What did you mean, then? Is there something wrong with me?" she asked shakily.

"No! No, of course there isn't." Her mum hugged her fiercely, pulling Emily into her arms and squeezing her so tight she could hardly breathe. "You're feeling weird because you've got a bug, I should think. You're perfect. And I love you."

Emily hugged her back. She was fairly sure her mum was telling her the truth. But there was still something strange going on. Mum hadn't answered her question either.

But Emily didn't want to ask it again. She wanted to be fussed over, and told that everything was all right. If she saw something in the mirror, or the pictures on the stairs spoke to her, or people stared at her out of books, she wasn't going to look. If she didn't look, she couldn't see. And right now, that was the way she wanted it.

✳

Emily stayed away from the library at school, and she refused to look at the mirror on the landing. It was hard not to think about all the odd stuff that had been happening, but she could just about manage it. Robin was her annoying little brother, that was all. She'd had a bug. Gruff stayed sleeping on Emily's bed at night, and Emily hardly dreamed at all.

It was tempting, though. She longed to go and look at the book again. What if someone else borrowed it? What if it got lost? It had a scary fascination, like that strange picture book about goblins that she'd loved when she was little. She could only look at it in the cupboard under the stairs, which was small and dark and smelled musty, but it was safe. It was probably still there, stuffed behind Lark's old roller skates, Emily thought as she wandered down the stairs on Saturday morning, with Gruff thudding from step to step behind her.

She came into the kitchen yawning, and stopped, realizing that her mother and father had gone silent when they saw her.

"What?" Emily pulled her hoodie top tighter round her shoulders, wrapping it round her like a comfort blanket.

Her mother blinked, and smiled. "Don't look so suspicious, Ems. I was just saying it would be nice to have a family dinner tonight. All of us together. It seems ages since we managed to get us all in one place."

"Oh. . ." Emily nodded. She looked hopefully

at her mother. "Can I make some of the food? Can I make pudding? Please, Mum?" Emily couldn't imagine anything nicer than spending the day pottering about the kitchen, leafing through recipe books and mixing up delicious stuff. After all the oddness of this week, it would feel like being normal again.

Her mother smiled at her and gently pushed a pile of recipe books across the table. The kitchen table was huge, and as everyone had been rushing in and out all week, no one had needed to clear it properly so they could all sit down. Emily slid into a chair and started to leaf through the book on the top – full of beautiful photos of cakes. She did cook savoury things sometimes – she was good at pasta – but cakes were her favourite

92

thing to cook. There was something magical about the way the ingredients went together and looked like a weird sort of gloop, but then the heat of the oven turned them into something new and different.

Magical – Emily shivered, and scowled at the chocolate brownie recipe she was reading. It wasn't magic. It was just cooking. Maybe a bit of science. Chemical reactions and that sort of thing. Everything worked the way it was supposed to; it was just a matter of following the recipe.

But recipes didn't work for some people. Mum's cakes never rose properly, and she loved to tell the story about Lark begging for shop cake when she and Lory were little, because Mummy's biscuits were horrible. When they'd had a cake sale at school and Emily had made chocolate raspberry brownies, Mrs Daunt had told her she had a magic touch.

Emily slammed the book shut, her breathing fast and panicky. She would not think about it!

"What did that recipe ever do to you?" her dad asked mildly, peering at her over a sheaf of papers. "Are you busy, Emily? Will you read this for me?" Then he shook his head. "Actually, no. You don't need to. It's terrible. If your mother comes back, tell her I'm working, all right?" He gathered up the papers and hurried out of the room, muttering irritably to himself.

Emily nodded, glad that he'd been distracted.

She opened up a different recipe book, determined not to think about magic at all.

Soon she was too busy to think about anything but her plan – a new recipe that she'd come up with for a sort of lemon caramel cake, with crystallized rose petals decorating the top. It borrowed bits of about five different recipes, and it was very complicated. So complicated that she hadn't been able to worry about the last week while she was making it, she realized as she carefully scattered the flower petals on the top of her finished creation. It was nearly time for everyone to have dinner. She sighed, feeling as though she could breathe properly for the first time in days – there wasn't a hard little knot in her throat any more, blocking the air. She felt full of sugar dust instead, and her hair smelled of caramel.

"Emily, it's so pretty." Lory touched a rose petal with one delicate finger. "It's OK! I'm not eating it! Just looking!"

Emily smiled at her. "It is pretty, isn't it? Almost too nice to eat, but I really want to know what it tastes like. And I'm starving."

"Yes, well, you would be!" her mum pointed out. "When I asked you if you wanted lunch you told me you couldn't possibly stop because you were in the middle of the tricky bit with your caramel, and after that I didn't dare interrupt."

Emily leaned against her for a second, sliding her arm round her mum's waist. "Sorry. I forgot about lunch. I did eat a few rose petals, but that

96

explains why I feel totally empty."

"Well, I just about managed to fit the roast chicken in round your cake. It should all be done, I think."

"My favourite." Emily sighed happily. Her mum might be useless at cakes, but her roast potatoes were legendary. Emily gave the scattering of petals on top of her cake a last dusting of icing sugar and grabbed a handful of cutlery to set the table. Her dad was fussing around finding matches to light candles, and Lark and Lory had picked flowers and twined ivy up the middle of the table. It felt like a really important occasion.

But as everyone sat down in the glimmering candlelight, Emily felt strangely shy. It was as

97

though the beautiful table and the special food made it hard to talk. There were odd silences, broken only by admiring comments on how good the food was. Emily's mum kept saying how nice it was to sit down as a family, and how special it felt. But the more she said it, the more forced it sounded.

Even though roast chicken was her absolute favourite meal, Emily didn't feel hungry. She nibbled a roast potato and sneaked a few bits of chicken down to Gruff, who was leaning lovingly against her ankles. Chicken was Gruff's favourite too. Emily was pretty sure that Lark and Lory were feeding him on the other side of the table as well. He was big enough to beg from both sides at once.

Eventually, Robin laid down his fork with a sharp ring of metal on china, and glared at Eva and Ash.

"Can we just tell her, please?"

5

"Robin!" Lory hissed.

"It's stupid. We're going to tell her anyway; why do we have to do all this polite talking about nothing? Nobody's saying anything important. You and Lark were talking about your favourite colour for flowers! And no one's eating any dinner."

"There's a time for these things," Ash murmured.

"We were waiting. . ."

"Well, I'm bored waiting."

Emily sat staring at them all, her eyes flicking back and forth between Robin, who was sitting next to her, and the others. "What were you going to tell me?" she asked huskily. Her voice didn't seem to be working properly. Apart from Robin, who was sticking his bottom lip out in a sulk, everyone looked so serious. Something was wrong, Emily was sure. Maybe her mum and dad were splitting up? But why would they tell everyone else and not her? Why have a meal that was meant to be all about family and then break it up? It couldn't be that.

"What is it?" she asked again.

Lark, who was sitting next to her, leaned over

and put an arm round Emily's shoulder, pressing her cool cheek against Emily's for a second. Then she stood up, and across the table Lory stood as well.

Emily stared at her sisters, her heart thudding. The strangeness in the room seemed to shiver on her skin – everyone was tense and keyed up, waiting for something.

Lark smiled at her, and then she twisted her shoulders in some strange way, and feathers poured out of her back, soft grey-brown feathers, with darker stripes and mottles. Wings. Lark looked like an angel, Emily thought, gazing at her.

Or a fairy. Her sister's skin was shining, with the same strange glimmer as that girl by the river.

She *had* been a fairy. Of course she had. Emily should never have doubted it.

Emily's fingers twitched, longing to stroke the soft feathers. She thought they were the most beautiful thing she'd ever seen. Usually brown was a boring sort of colour, but Lark's feathers glowed in the candlelight. They seemed to be dusted with a shimmering layer of magic, swirling into ever-changing patterns like oil on water. They were so hypnotic, Emily almost forgot to breathe.

"You can touch them," Lark told her, smiling, and Emily nodded. But she didn't touch. She didn't dare.

Lark stretched her wings out a little further, fluttering them from her shoulders and smiling at Emily. The way she smiled was as if she was teasing Emily with a bit of her chocolate. "Go on. You know you want to."

Emily sighed, a tiny breath out, and lifted her hand. It was trembling, and she could only bring herself to stroke one finger down Lark's wing.

The magic buzzed inside her as she touched the feathers. The whole earth was suddenly swinging sickeningly around her, even though she was standing still. It was like a rollercoaster ride. She'd always loved scary rides. It was blissful.

"Emily, look at me. . ." a sweet voice purred, and Emily dragged herself away from the feathers and turned to stare at Lory. Then she watched the weird transformation all over again. Lory closed her eyes and shivered her shoulders, and the feathers rushed out in a fall of orange and crimson and gold. The wings stretched out like Lark's, shimmering in the candlelight. The same but different – scarlet feathers that clashed with Lory's golden-yellow hair but still looked beautiful. The same way Lory could put on an old skirt and a top that clashed and look amazing. Emily had always said enviously to herself that it was like magic. Now she gave a squeaky little gulp of laughter. She'd never thought it really was.

"Now look at *me*," Robin demanded, reaching out a hand across the table – a hand with impossibly long fingers. Why hadn't Emily ever realized that before? Robin twisted his fingers, pulling her eyes up to his face, making her stare.

105

He had wings too, she could see them behind his back, but it was his pointed ears that he wanted her to see, and the strange angle of his silvery eyes.

"Emily. . ." Her mother was kneeling next to her chair, and Emily gasped as she turned to look into her face. It was still her mother – Emily recognized her – but she was so different. Her hair was even fierier than it had been before, and it crackled out around her face like a halo, glittering with power and magic. Her silver-grey eyes filled half her face now, and they seemed to swirl like great pools of water. Emily gazed at her, entranced, swaying a little as she was wrapped in her mother's charming spell.

A cool hand stroked her cheek, and Emily

106

turned, blinking, and looked into her father's eyes. She recognized them, even though they were darker, blacker, than they'd ever seemed to be before.

Ash. . . Emily could see why that was his name. His skin was grey and soft, with just the faintest hint of feathering that traced across his cheeks and into his white and silver hair. He was the strangest of all of them – the least human.

For it was obvious now. They weren't human. None of her family were.

"Are you – are you fairies?" Emily whispered.

Robin rolled his eyes. He still seemed very much her little brother, even though he had soft brown wings sprouting from his shoulders.

"Well, what do you think, Emily? What else would we be?"

Emily suddenly forgot to be entranced by his shining eyes and the glow of magic all around him. He'd been using his magic, messing around and translocating her to places. He'd been lying to her. He might be some sort of fairy, but he was still himself. And still annoying. "I don't know," she said, smirking a little. "You could be a gnome. They're the little ones, aren't they? Shorty."

"I'm not!" Robin yelled, and the faint glitter of magic coming off his skin got brighter, as though he was about to explode. Their dad put a warning hand on his shoulder.

Emily folded her arms and sniggered. She couldn't resist teasing him just a bit more. "Maybe a pixie?" Then she shook her head. "Sorry. . . I suppose all those things are real too. There really are pixies. And, um, sprites, and elves. . ." She looked at her mum, the long red hair rippling down her back like flames. She could see every strand of it, all glittering, and it *moved*. Eva looked like an elf – like Emily imagined an elf would look from the stories she'd read, anyway. Tall, and grand, and as if she'd be scary if she wasn't actually Emily's mum as well.

"You're all fairies. . ." she said slowly. "Our whole family is. So I must be – something." Emily let out an excited gasp of laughter, and looked down at herself. She was hoping to see feathers, or at least her black hair grown longer and shinier, like magic. But it hadn't happened yet. Maybe she was still growing into it, and that was why they'd wanted to tell her. So she was ready. She nodded to herself. She definitely was.

"Is this why all the strange things have been happening? The dreams? Because I'm changing too? Why didn't you tell me till now, though?"

Then she smiled – she didn't really care why it had taken so long. She wasn't just seeing things. She was a fairy! It explained everything: all the odd things she'd been seeing, and the weird way the house behaved. She twisted her fingers together, trying to stop herself laughing. It was all so right. Everything made sense at last. She giggled suddenly. What was she going to tell Rachel?

"It doesn't matter that you didn't tell me,"

she added quickly. "I just wondered. Will I have wings? You and Dad don't, so why do Lark and Lory and Robin all have them?" Then she swallowed, a sudden tide of happiness rising up inside her. "Can you *fly*?" she asked, whirling round to catch Lark's hand.

"Yes," Lark whispered, but she didn't look very happy about it. Her wings had faded a little, and stopped shining, and they were folded flat against her back, tucked up against her purple vest top. Her fingers felt chilly in Emily's hand.

Emily looked at her worriedly. "Are you OK? I don't mind if I don't have wings, honestly."

"Oh, Emily. . ." Her mum put her hand to her mouth.

Ash let go of Robin, and Robin wasn't looking

111

furious any more. He looked – sad.

"What is it?" Emily asked, feeling suddenly scared. She let go of Lark and stepped back, staring at them all anxiously. "Is there something wrong with me?" she whispered. "Is that why it's taken so long for me to change?"

Her dad came round the table and caught both her hands, holding them tight in his own. They felt soft, and feathery, and very strong. "Emily, little one. You don't understand. You aren't like us."

Emily shook her head. "A different sort of fairy?" she asked, but her voice was husky and breaking.

"No."

"But why?" Emily's eyes burned with tears.

How could she be a fairy's child, without any magic of her own? It didn't make sense. "It – it isn't fair," she stammered. "How can you all be magical and I'm not? It can't happen that way." She looked round at the rest of her family, all watching her with huge, shining eyes. Lark and Lory had tears glittering on their cheeks, and Lark rubbed one graceful hand across her face. Emily gulped. Fairies never did anything so ugly as sniffing.

"Maybe it's just taking a long time to show," she added, trying to sound hopeful. "I have to be like you. I'm your daughter." She gazed pleadingly up at Ash, gripping his strange hands too tightly.

Eva was standing next to him now, and Emily could feel Lark and Lory on either side of her, the feathery warmth of their wings wrapping around her.

"Emily, you're not," Ash said gently.

There was silence as Emily looked at him, trying desperately to make those words not mean what they said. She couldn't.

"Not yours? I don't understand. I *am* your daughter. . . You know I am," Emily whispered. It didn't make sense – except that in an awful sort of way, it did make sense of a lot of things. "I don't believe you," she said, trying to sound strong, but it didn't work. She swallowed, her mouth dry and papery. "Who am I, then?"

Ash glanced at Eva, who sighed. "We don't know, Emily," she whispered.

Emily shook her head. It was like touching

Lark's wings all over again – the ground seemed to be swinging and shaking underneath her, except this time it didn't feel magical and exciting. It was awful. Her whole life had gone wobbly, and everything she knew about herself was wrong. "How can you not know?" she begged. "You have to know! Where did I come from if I'm not yours?" She pulled her hands away from Ash, wrapping them around her middle as though it might help her hold together.

Her dad – not her dad at all, Emily thought miserably – reached out for her, and she took another step back, tipping over her chair and pressing up against the wall. He dropped his hands and gazed at her sadly, his dark eyes glinting black in the candlelight. "Don't be scared, Emily. Maybe we should have told you sooner, but we wanted you to be old enough to understand."

"I'm not scared!" Emily told him shakily. But she was. "I don't understand. I'm *not* old enough to understand, I couldn't be. Where did I come from?"

"I found you," Ash told her quietly.

"Where? When?" Emily demanded, her voice rising in panic.

Eva reached out a hand, and Emily could see that her fingers were blurring and glittering, as though they were surrounded with magic. But Ash stopped her, gently pushing her hand away. "Don't. . . She needs to know all of this – and she's right to be upset."

"Where did you find me? Who do I belong to?"

"You belong to us!" Eva almost howled it, but Ash was shaking his head.

"I found you. . ." He faltered, and then started again. "I found you by the river, and I brought you home."

Emily gaped at him. That couldn't be true. It sounded like a fairy tale, she thought to herself – and then swallowed a laugh. "You just *took* me?" she asked him disbelievingly.

Ash nodded helplessly, and Emily felt her legs give way. She slid slowly down so that she was sitting against the wall and gazed up at them all, standing over her.

They'd stolen her.

6

Emily rubbed her hand across her face. There was so much she didn't understand.

"Didn't anyone notice that you suddenly had an extra baby?" she murmured. "What did you tell people?"

Ash crouched down in front of her. "We didn't tell anyone anything, Emily love."

"Oh. . ." Emily nodded slowly. "I suppose you

can just make people believe anything?"

"Pretty much."

"But we don't," Eva put in. "Only when we really have to. We try to live without our magic as much as we can, while we're here."

"You could do anything . . . anything you like." Emily felt her eyes filling with tears. "What did you want me for? What use could I be to someone like you?"

Ash frowned. "I don't know, Emily. I wasn't thinking like that. I couldn't leave you there, that's all."

"But what about my real parents?" Emily gulped. "Did you – did you leave something else behind?"

Then it hit Emily with a sudden force, almost

119

stealing away her breath. The book. This was why Robin had to get her out of the library. They didn't want her reading that book, because she might remember what had happened.

She was the girl. The stolen baby in the story of the changeling child. Except – the fairies hadn't taken her to some distant fairy land, they'd kept her here. The wooden baby from the story filled her mind, leering at her with its strange, sharp-toothed smile. What if her real parents hadn't known, and that changeling baby was still living in her room, taking Emily's place in her true family?

"She means a changeling," Robin said. He was sitting on the edge of the table, his wings twitching idly behind him. "She was reading that story, remember? It wasn't like that, Emily."

"I didn't steal you," Ash said, stroking her cheek, the way he always did when she was sad. In spite of herself, even knowing what he had done, Emily felt better. It wasn't a spell, she was almost sure. It was just her dad being lovely.

How could he not be her father? Emily's tears spilled down over Ash's fingers, and he flinched a little, his lips pulling back over pointed teeth. But he kept going, gently cradling her face and talking to her.

"I didn't have to steal you, Emily. You were on your own. Someone had left you there, by the river. Wrapped up in a blanket. I couldn't leave you there. Like you said, I just – took you."

"He went out for a walk and came back with

you," Lark said, patting her knee. "When he brought you home, we thought you were a doll. We were only three, and you were tiny, Emily. Doll-sized."

"I was abandoned?" Emily asked, her voice hardly above a whisper. "They didn't want me?"

"But we wanted you," Eva said fiercely. "We still do. We shouldn't have told her," she added in a murmur to Ash. "We were all so happy. . ."

Emily sprang up, pushing her way past Ash, and feeling the jolt of magic as his power caught at her. "You should!" she sobbed. "You were happy, but it was all a lie. I knew it was. I could feel it. I didn't fit in. I'm not yours! You shouldn't ever have taken me in the first place."

Emily darted out of the kitchen door, racing

122

for the stairs. All she could think of was to get away to her room, to think. To work out what she was going to do. To try and understand what was going on.

How could she not have realized before? She didn't look like Robin and Lory and Lark. She wasn't brilliant at school like they were. There were so many ways that she didn't fit in. But she'd thought that meant she was just the odd one out – not that she didn't belong to her family at all.

It was just too much stuff to take in. She needed her room, and her things. She wanted to wrap herself up in her quilt and think about it all. Lark and Lory and Robin had wings – they could really fly. Who knew what else they could

123

do? Her mum had said they tried to live without magic as much as possible, but maybe Robin and Lark and Lory did it all the time? She smiled miserably to herself. It would explain why Robin always managed to do his homework in about three minutes flat.

Emily blinked and looked around her. She had been blindly rushing up to her room, her eyes so full of tears that she wasn't really looking where she was going. Now she was halfway up the stairs, and she could tell that something was wrong.

She was cold, and the stairs smelled weird. Emily clutched the banisters, and sniffed, and rubbed her hand across her eyes.

The stairs were growing. The wooden spindles

that held the banisters up were sprouting thin little branches and tiny leaves. As she watched, the leaf buds opened out into delicate fans of green. The banister felt rough under her fingers, like bark.

Emily closed her eyes, and opened them again. Was this her mum and dad – Ash and Eva, she corrected herself sadly – using their magic to bring her back downstairs? *Honestly, they could have just shouted*, she thought. But then, they probably had. She hadn't been listening.

Emily shook her head angrily. She wanted time on her own. They couldn't spring something like this on her and expect her not to be upset!

Determinedly, she marched up the last few

125

steps to the landing. If she tried hard enough, she could see through the magic to the real stairs. They were still there, even though she seemed to be climbing a hill with short, sheep-nibbled grass, and rocky slabs laid into it to climb up.

"It's a spell," Emily muttered, trying not to be delighted by the flowers growing over the stones. They smelled so beautiful, and their petals were jewel-bright. . . Emily hissed and shut her eyes again, climbing by feel. The stone slabs didn't feel like stone yet, though she suspected they might, if she wasn't quick.

She carefully didn't look into the mirror outside Lark's room, but she could see out of the corner of her eye that someone was moving inside it – or something. Emily stomped on with a grim determination to get inside her own room and slam the door on everybody else. When there weren't fairy sisters fluttering their magic wings at her and filling the air with spells, she would be able to *think*.

It felt as though she'd taken hours to get across the landing and over to the creaky little narrow staircase to her room. She would not let them drag her back! Emily braced both hands against the walls and half pulled herself upwards. She risked a glance behind through half-closed eyes, and set her teeth. More branches. Twined with dark, glossy ivy now, woven in and out with trails of tiny white flowers that smelled of honey.

"I don't like honey, Mum," Emily snarled. "You ought to know." *I bet you would know, if I was*

really yours, she added silently, hot tears burning her eyes again.

The ivy was wrapping itself around her fingers, wiry stems pulling her in. Emily yanked her hands away, seeing the leaves shiver and rattle in surprise. "Stop it! I'm going up to my room, leave me alone!" She put her hands on to the step in front of her, going on all fours instead, clinging to the steps with her fingertips, even though they groaned and gave underneath her. She was not climbing up a thin lattice of branches, Emily told herself determinedly. It was an illusion. There were stairs underneath, solid ones, and she would not give in.

With a triumphant gasp, she reached up and grabbed the white china door handle – she wasn't even going to think about what that might be turning into. Her door was glowing; the purple paint she'd chosen had turned translucent, like the amethysts in Eva's favourite necklace. Emily just hauled the door open and slammed it behind her. "Leave me alone!" she yelled, leaning back against the door and closing her eyes.

It was when she opened them again that Emily first thought she might have made a mistake. She had assumed that once she got inside her room, the magic from downstairs would stop. Her mum and dad would stop, she'd thought. They'd give up and let her have some time on her own.

But the strange purple glow of the door was just the same on the other side – brighter, if anything. She could see it shining through her

129

fingers where they were pressed against the door – the same way that they glowed red if she cupped a torch inside her hand. Except this light was brighter, and stronger, and it had the same honey-flower smell as the tiny blossoms on her stairs.

It didn't make her think of Ash, or Eva, or her sisters. And Robin definitely wouldn't make something like this. Downstairs, even when Eva had looked so odd, with those huge eyes and her fiery hair, she had still felt like herself to Emily. Lark's wings had been part of Lark. Emily was pretty sure, now that she thought about it, surrounded by this weird, sickly-sweet glow, that she would know a spell that any of them had made.

This was something else. And she wasn't in her bedroom at all.

Emily swallowed and let go of the door. She recognized this. The odd purple cast over everything had made it look different, but the purple light was fading now, and she could tell it was the riverbank that she'd seen in her dream.

It was darker now, but she recognized it. And even though it was dark, it seemed more real. Clearer. She was actually here, she realized. She shivered a little as a chill rose off the water and rustled the leaves on the willow trees. This was no dream.

She had gone *through* that purple door to somewhere else. It wasn't like the stairs, where she could see the real steps beneath the magic.

This was another world.

She glanced behind at her bedroom door, wondering how she'd managed to get here when it should have been her room. Then she let out a little moan of panic.

Her door wasn't there now either. No more weird purple light. The door had disappeared when she let go of it.

Emily stepped forward, making for the very edge of the water, where she'd met the girl with the weed-green hair in her dream. The girl had been friendly – or friendly-ish, at least. She might tell Emily where she was. And how she was supposed to get back home, now that the door had gone.

7

Emily crept forward, pushing her way through the dangling branches of the willow trees, straining her eyes in the dim, greenish light. It was very eerie. But then, anything would be after the way she'd arrived here, she told herself. It didn't necessarily mean bad things.

The trees were swaying, the long leafy trails swinging in the wind. Emily lifted up a handful of leaves and gasped, finding a pale-faced boy staring back at her, smiling. He had the same huge-eyed, sharp-eared look as Robin, but his hair was distinctly green, and Emily was sure that if he leaned back against the willow-tree trunk, his grey-brown skin and the dusty-looking trousers he was wearing would disappear, melting into the bark.

"I – I don't know where I am. . ." Emily faltered. "I didn't mean to come – here. Um. I don't actually know where here is. Could you show me – I mean, the door's gone. . ."

The boy smiled wider, and put his finger to his lips.

"Oh! Oh, sorry. . ."

This time, he pressed his finger to Emily's lips

instead, and then there was a strange hissing sound from all around her. Emily glanced sideways, and gasped. There were at least ten or so more girls and boys, a little older than her. All touching her, and cooing, and purring, and patting at her gently, as though she were a baby, or a kitten.

The original green-haired boy looked disgruntled, she thought, as though he hadn't really wanted to share. He was at the back of the little huddle now, his lips crossly pursed, and his hands resting on his bony hips.

What did they want from her? Emily thought in a panic, as the strong, silky fingers ran over her hair and pulled at the sleeves of her hoodie. Anxiously, she started to pull away, or try to, but there were too many of them, wafting their scented hair in her face, and purring at her in words she almost recognized. Words that she'd heard Eva singing, or Lark and Lory, before Ash told them to be quiet. Emily had thought it was because he was working, but maybe he just didn't want her to hear. Their voices were very sweet. . .

She stared at them vaguely, trying to remember what was happening, but all she could think was that they were fairies, like her sisters, and that Lark and Lory and the rest of her family probably spoke like this too. When she wasn't around. It was the saddest thing she'd ever imagined, and tears puddled in the corners of her eyes and ran down her cheeks.

There was an outbreak of whispering at that, as the fairies followed the tracks of her tears with their fingertips, and one daring girl with brown hair all wound up with twigs touched a tear, and winced, and then licked her finger, laughing.

Did human tears burn? Emily wondered. Ash had flinched at the touch of them as well. At least, she thought he had. Her memories were fading and blurring as the fairies whispered in her ears and stroked her hair so gently. She began to feel herself swaying, and now her thoughts were only of how beautiful they were, their large eyes gleaming as they stared down at her.

"Ssshhh, ssshhh," they whispered, as she sank back into their arms, and they carried her off, singing.

137

Emily blinked, and groaned a little. Her head was aching. And Mum must have found a new fabric conditioner, because her bed smelled really weird, too sweet and flowery. Someone was sitting on the bed with her – Emily guessed it was Gruff, and reached out a hand to stroke him sleepily.

The someone laughed, and Emily jumped up, jolted awake in a second. In that moment between sleeping and waking, she had forgotten what had happened, what she knew now.

Was she dreaming, maybe? For one last hopeful instant she wondered if it had *all* been a dream – that when she was properly awake, she'd be able to go into her parents' room, and tell them she'd dreamed they were all fairies, and she was adopted. Perhaps her dad would laugh at her, and say it was a sign, and it must mean she ought to make him some fairy cakes; they were his favourite.

But she was properly awake already. She knew she was. She pinched the back of her hand just in case, and then sucked at it, because it hurt.

The fairy sitting on the side of the huge bed tutted anxiously at her, and took Emily's hand in both of hers, shaking her head and murmuring at Emily soothingly. "Don't do that, silly child."

Emily frowned, puzzled. "Have I met you before? I feel like I have, but I can't have done. . ."

The girl smiled at her. She was much grander-looking than the greenish people Emily had met on the riverbank. Emily guessed that perhaps they were tree spirits, given their leafy, bark-skinned look. This girl looked more like Eva, or maybe Lory, with a mass of golden-bright hair, intricately wreathed and plaited around her head. Jewelled wires were woven in and out of the coils, so that the whole of her hair resembled some amazing, delicate crown. She had wings like Lark and Lory too, but hers were more like a butterfly's, a soft, dusty, pale green scattered with black spots and frills all round the edges. Her dress was a stronger green than her wings, and it was embroidered all over in golden thread, scattered here and there with jewelled flowers.

Emily swallowed sadly. It looked very like something her mother would have made. But of course it did. This was where all Eva's wild, beautiful designs had come from. And probably Ash's eerie novels too, Emily thought. She shivered. She hoped that not all the strange monsters he'd come up with were real.

Emily lifted her eyes from the fairy's dress to her face, carefully, trying hard not to look her in the eyes. She wasn't quite sure why – it just seemed to be a good idea.

"I'm not meant to be here," Emily said awkwardly, looking at the girl's pointed ears, her jewelled hair, anywhere but her dark, sparkling eyes. "It was an accident."

"Oh, I'm sure you *should* be here," the fairy disagreed. "Nothing ever really happens by accident, does it?" She ran delicate, soft fingers down the side of Emily's cheek. "So pretty. So alive! It only amazes me, Emily, that you haven't found your way here before."

There was a chorus of pretty, jingling laughter at this, and Emily realized that she and the fairy weren't alone in the room. Somehow she hadn't been able to see past her until now. But it was as if the laughter broke a spell, and Emily could see that there was a cluster of other beautiful girls around the bed, their hair woven into different elaborate styles, and their dresses just as fine.

Two more of them, one in a rose pink dress, the other wearing a dark crimson-red that picked up the purplish lights in her black hair, came to sit on the bed next to Emily.

"We've been longing to meet you," the dark-

142

haired girl whispered. "We've seen glimpses of you, through the doors. We've wanted to meet you properly for so long. . ."

Emily blinked at her. "I don't understand. . ." she murmured. "Which doors? I don't know you, I'm sure I don't. How do you know my name?"

"Ohhh, she looks exhausted, poor little thing," the girl in pink murmured, her gauzy dragonfly wings shimmering excitedly. "We should be more hospitable, don't you think?"

"Of course, how rude we are. . ." The fairy girl in green laughed again. "You must be hungry, Emily." She waved a hand, a sharp commanding movement that didn't seem to sit well with her graceful air.

Emily swallowed, her eyes widening. It was

as if the fairy's gesture suddenly made the rest of the room appear. Until then, Emily had only seen the bed she was lying on, and the fairies gathered close to it. The bed was strange enough, a careless bundle of grand fabrics and coverlets slung over a gilded frame. The bedposts were clearly metal, but so delicately twisted into the shapes of flowers and birds and tiny mice that they could have been alive. Perhaps they had been, once. That little golden frog's look of wide-eyed surprise could well be real.

But now Emily gazed out across the room, as a tiny creature wrapped in brown approached her with a plate. It was the largest bedroom she'd ever been in, even bigger than Rachel's gorgeous room. It looked like a room in the castle they'd

144

been to last year on their school trip, with a polished stone floor and bright tapestries hanging on the walls.

Waiting by the door of the room was a little cluster of smaller creatures, like the one who was holding out the plate to her now. Servants, Emily thought, from their clothes and their bowed heads. She looked curiously at the fairy offering her the food, wondering if they were all children, or if they were just some smaller sort of fairy. Gnomes, maybe, she wondered, remembering what she'd said to Robin. Or perhaps brownies. Brownies made her smile, and think of Rachel again – Rach had been a Brownie, and she'd loved it. Emily had never gone, mostly because Lark and Lory hadn't, and when she'd been smaller, she'd wanted to be just like them.

That was never going to happen now, Emily thought, blinded by sudden tears again as she remembered. She wrapped her arms around her knees and hugged them tight.

The brownie, or whatever it was, stared up at her in horror, as though it thought it might be blamed for her unhappiness. It was a girl, Emily decided. Something about the wide, golden-brown face made her sure, though it was hard to tell. The snub nose and dark, dark eyes could be either a boy's or a girl's, and so could the tousled hair. She wore a plain brown tunic, with a twist of ivy wrapped around the waist for a belt. Her hands were shaking, Emily suddenly realized, feeling sorry for her. Perhaps she really was going to get into trouble. The little creature lifted up the plate to her again, staring at her hopefully, and Emily caught the smell of the fruit that was spilling over the sides.

For a moment she forgot how frightened she was, and how angry with her family. She'd never smelled anything so good – except, perhaps, a long time ago, at home. Something a little like it once, when she'd been playing with Lark and Lory in the garden. She couldn't remember quite where.

The pieces of fruit seemed to glow against the silver plate, as though they were lit from inside: a cluster of emerald-green berries, and something that looked like an orange, except it was split open down one side, spilling out scarlet seeds, dripping with juice. And apples, golden and fawn and green, glossy leaves still attached, as though they'd been picked only moments before.

Emily stretched out her hand to take something without even meaning to, and the brownie let out a sigh, as though she hadn't dared to breathe before, and smiled at her, nodding eagerly. She balanced the plate in one hand, and with the other, she held out a fine cloth napkin to Emily, as though she had on one of those beautiful jewelled dresses that might be ruined by a smear of juice, and not just her denim shorts and a hoodie.

"Do eat, Emily," the dark-haired fairy murmured eagerly, her eyes sparkling. She reached out to the plate and took an apple while the brownie watched her nervously. Her small, pointed teeth bit into it deeply, and she sighed. "So good. You should try." The juice was running down her chin a little, and she licked it away. Then she closed her eyes, and her wings quivered in delight. The peacock eyes in the corners shimmered, the colours pulsing, so that Emily could only stare at them, and be filled with hunger for the sweet fruit.

Which to choose? Emily took the napkin with a murmured, "Thank you," and reached out, stroking the sun-warmed fruit. She had just picked up a strand of garnet-red berries when there was a sudden commotion at the door. The other brownies were shrieking in alarm, and the brownie girl holding out the plate to her turned

149

round, shrinking back against the bed anxiously.

"Emily, no!"

Lark and Lory were racing towards her, weirdly out of place in their jeans and vest tops, their feathered wings spilling out behind them as they ran.

The dark-haired fairy with the peacock butterfly wings gasped angrily. She dropped the apple, standing up hurriedly in a rustle of stiff silk skirts as though she meant to stop Lark and Lory coming anywhere near. But the other two fairies caught her hands, whispering to her, and she sat down, watching with a strange sort of smile.

Emily's first reaction was to leap off the bed and hug her sisters – she was so glad to see

150

someone she knew in this strange, terrifying, beautiful place. She reached out to Lark, smiling in relief. Then she remembered.

Lark and Lory belonged here, just as much as the fairy girls in their finery. Emily didn't. She stared at them doubtfully.

"Don't eat anything!" Lory snapped, reaching out a hand for the berries, and Lark snatched the plate from the frightened brownie and flung it on to the ground. The servant girl let out a little wail of horror, and the other fairies whispered angrily to each other.

"Why not?" Emily pulled away, feeling suddenly cross, and clutched the handful of berries against her top. Lark and Lory always ordered her about – and they weren't even her sisters. "What did you do that for? She was only being nice!"

Lark sighed, and reached out to put an arm round her, but Emily pulled away, scrambling up the bed with the berries still in her hand. She could feel the other fairies watching eagerly, and the one with the peacock wings was leaning over to her now, holding out her own hands and smiling, as though she wanted to wrap Emily in her arms and comfort her.

"Nice!" Lory laughed in disgust. "Emily, don't be stupid! If you eat, you'll have to stay here! You can't eat fairy fruit and go back to your own world; you'll never want to eat real food again. It'll taste like ashes, and you'll starve, pining for just one more taste of those berries."

152

Lark nodded, her eyes bluer than ever, glittering with worried tears.

"Don't listen to them, Emily," the fairy in the green dress said sweetly. "Why would you want to go back, anyway? Stay here with us. We won't lie to you."

Emily hesitated, looking back and forth between the fairy girls and Lark and Lory. Her sisters looked even more fairy-like here, their wings and hair sparkling with a furious light.

"Emily," Lark tried again, her voice gentle but shakily anxious. "Emily, you don't understand. They want to steal you. They won't let you go home."

Emily swallowed, trying to make the ache in her chest go away. "It isn't really my home," she

153

told Lark miserably. "Is it? And I've already been stolen. . ." With a weary sort of stubbornness, she pulled a berry off the little cluster in her hand and reached up to put it in her mouth.

There was an excited hiss of indrawn breath from the fairy girls around her, and Lark screamed, "Emily, look!"

Jolted out of her anger by the pure fear in Lark's eyes, Emily looked where she was pointing. At the fruit that Lark had thrown across the floor. It was scattered over the polished stone, brown and wizened-looking, the scarlet seeds of that strange fruit all over the floor now, smearing the stone with a blackish, treacly juice.

Emily glanced down at the berries in her hand and flung them away in horror. They'd shrivelled to an ugly mess, seeping and covered in a grey-blue mould. She had been about to eat that. . .

"Emily, come on, please. We have to go. Just trust us, please." Lory was holding out her hand. She had glittery nail polish on, and it was flaking a bit. Real nail varnish, the one that Emily had borrowed off her a week or so before, without asking. The glitter was made of little plasticky flecks, not some lying, beautiful magic.

Slowly, Emily reached out, and put her hand in her sister's.

8

Someone screamed in fury, and Emily looked back at the fairy girls gathered around the bed. Their faces had changed – they were still beautiful, but now they looked paler and older, and almost cruel, their features sharp with rage.

"Don't let her go!" the dark-haired fairy cried, and the little brownie servant caught at Emily's sleeve.

"You're not having her," Lory snapped, yanking Emily away, so that the brownie fell back against the bed. She pulled Emily behind her, putting herself between Emily and the fairy girls. They were calling for the servants to fetch help, and the dark-haired fairy was stepping delicately after them, still smiling, and beckoning to Emily.

"Emily, I know you think we lied, but we never wanted to hurt you." Lory stared at Emily for a second, and then ducked her eyes. "I don't want to charm you. I need you to come with us because you want to."

"That's why neither of us are looking at you," Lory added, catching Emily's other hand. "Will you come with us?"

Emily nodded. The dark-haired fairy had sharp

pointed nails like beetle claws, and her feet were the wrong shape in her embroidered slippers. Now that Emily could see her without all the charms, she walked as though her legs were bent the other way. And she was getting closer.

Lark and Lory might not really be her sisters, but they weren't scary.

"Yes. I'll come," she gasped, tightening her hands around theirs.

Lark and Lory flung one arm each around her waist, and all at once their wings shot out with a sharp sound like flapping sails. They beat them frantically back and forth, and Emily squeaked as she realized what was about to happen, and closed her eyes, holding on as tightly as she could.

158

Flying didn't feel like she'd thought it would. It was bumpy, and noisy, and not at all graceful. But that was mostly because Lark and Lory were trying to do it together. The sound of them squabbling was so reassuring that Emily opened her eyes, discovered she was somewhere up near the ceiling, and shut them again.

"Window!" Lory snarled.

"We won't get out of it," Lark yelled back. "Too small!"

"We can squash – didn't you hear them calling? They've sent for huntsmen to chase us, Lory; we can't go back the way we came."

"Why don't they just chase us themselves?" Emily asked shakily. She had her eyes open now; she was just trying not to look down. "What are

159

they hunting for? I don't understand!"

"They're hunting you! And this lot can't chase us. Too old, too grand, and too lazy," Lark said grimly. "Come on."

"When we get back, Emily, you have to stop making cakes. We're all too fat for that window," Lory muttered as they swooped sickeningly towards it.

"We're never going to fit through that!" Emily wailed, looking at the tiny leaded window, opening on to a tangle of honeysuckle and jasmine.

"Just close your eyes and wish, Emily! We're fairies, remember!" Lark giggled, and Lory hissed crossly.

"So . . . it doesn't help if I wish, then?" Emily asked, just in case, watching Lark squish her wings smaller and wriggle frantically out of the window.

"No," Lory snapped. "And we can't use our magic here; it won't work. This is the fairy court, and it's guarded. Lark, hurry! They're coming!"

Lory shoved Emily towards the window frame, and she gulped, putting her knee up on the edge. It was all right. Lark was there to catch her. But it was all very well for Lark – she had wings, even though one of them was looking a bit battered by the squeeze out of the window. She was fluttering outside, beckoning anxiously to Emily. *She* wasn't going to fall.

"Ow!" Emily yelped, as Lory pushed her harder. "I'm going!"

"Hold on to the flowers!" Lark screamed, as

Emily half fell out of the window on top of her and they jolted downwards, pulling long trails of sweet-smelling flowers off the wall.

"Come on!" Lory shot past them and grabbed Emily's arm, yanking her up into the air so that she was dangling between her sisters. "We need to make for the river now, before those idiots work out where we're going and send someone to head us off."

Emily glanced back at the window, still surprised that they'd ever got out of it, and wondering if Lark and Lory had managed to use a spell after all.

Someone was leaning out of it now, staring after them. A young man with a bow in his hand and a sharp eager face. He was fitting an arrow to the string already, and Emily yelped.

"They wouldn't shoot us, would they?" Lory gasped. "They can't!"

"Fly faster," Emily gasped. "*Faster*, Lory. Stop talking."

"I'm – doing – my – best!" Lory panted, as they swooped and fluttered over ornamental gardens that reminded Emily of that castle again, and then over a ditch and into woodland, jinking through enormous, ancient trees.

"We're nearly at the river," Lark gasped, and they began to lose height, the frantic beating of Lark and Lory's wings slowing to a weary thud back and forth.

"Come on!"

Emily blinked wearily as the girl seemed to step

163

out of the shadows, her silvery dress suddenly shining in the greenish forest light. She was waving them on eagerly, and as they landed she caught Emily and reached out her arm to Lark, who was staggering, her wings drooping with weariness. "Run! I saw them. I was watching in the water, in the shining water."

"She can see things far away," Lory muttered to Emily, who was looking up and down the river anxiously. "She sees them in the water, sometimes."

"There's no time to tell her now!" The girl shook Lory's shoulder. "The Ladies' huntsmen are coming after you! Come on!"

Emily looked helplessly at Lark and Lory. It was the girl she'd met in her dream. The girl she'd seen in the mirror. Did they trust her? Was she a friend?

Lory nodded at the girl speechlessly. She was too out of breath to talk, Emily realized. Emily let the greenish girl haul her onwards, and together they staggered towards the river. She could see it glinting through the trees ahead.

"Where are we going? I'm not the best swimmer... Do we have to swim away from them?" she asked, staring worriedly at the fast-flowing water.

The water fairy shook her head, and her weed-like hair slapped against her shoulders. "It's a gate, Emily, a door. It'll take you home. Go on! Now!" She pulled Emily and Lark after her into the deepest part of the river. Emily whimpered at the cold bite of the water, and the awful feeling of the weeds sucking at her feet – pulling her down.

"Don't fight!" Lory gasped at her. "It's all right. Let go. . ."

And together they vanished under the water, streams of bubbles rising around them and hundreds of tiny startled faces peering at them through the weeds. Until they were standing on the wooden floorboards, on the landing, in Emily's house. And not even dripping.

"Ow. Ow, ow, ow, ow. . ." Lory sank down on to the floor, gently opening and closing her aching wings.

Emily huddled next to her, leaning against her shoulder and breathing in the warmth of Lory's feathers. She shook her head exhaustedly. "Where was that?" she muttered. "What happened? Who were those – the Ladies, she called them? And the huntsmen?"

There was a screech from downstairs, and then footsteps thundered out of the kitchen.

"Mum knows we're back." Lark flinched.

"They're going to kill us," Lory sighed, although she didn't sound all that worried.

Emily lifted her head up and looked at Lory. "Why?" Then her face crumpled. "Didn't they want me back?"

"Oh, Emily, shut up!" Lory poked her in the side. "Mum and Dad were terrified they'd lost you! They were trying to get you back quietly. Talking to the people who matter, on the other

167

side. Getting the Ladies to give you back, but without causing a big fuss. . ."

"But it was taking too long, we thought. Lory and me decided we'd get you ourselves," Lark said. She wrinkled her nose. "We were going to be quiet as well, but it didn't work out that way."

Emily snorted with laughter. "No." She was silent for a moment, letting Lark stroke her hair. "If you hadn't come and got me when you did, I'd probably have eaten the fruit."

"Mmm." Lark sighed.

"So . . . thanks. Even if you are the world's unsubtlest rescue party."

Eva flung herself up the last turn of the stairs and grabbed Emily, huddling over her and crying. It was strangely comforting, being wept over. No one could possibly think that Eva didn't want her. She was crying so much she could hardly speak.

Ash made up for that. He'd started shouting somewhere at the bottom of the stairs, and Lark and Lory were eyeing him warily as he stamped up and down the landing, turning back to yell how stupid they'd been, how dangerous it was, how they should have waited.

"You could have got Emily killed!" he thundered.

Lory sat up, hunching her wings high above her shoulders, like an angry hawk. "She was about to eat something! You were taking too long. We got her back, didn't we?"

Eva nodded, and swallowed, and managed to speak. "But it could have gone so much worse.

169

We could have lost all of you."

"The Ladies wouldn't have hurt us," Lark said, although she didn't sound very sure. After all, that huntsman had been notching an arrow.

"They might have got away with it, if it was only Emily. But they couldn't say they didn't know who we were."

Emily reached up and caught her father's hand as he paced furiously past. "Who's *they*? Who are these ladies? Where did I go?" She looked around at them, watching her in the shadows of the landing. They glowed, she noticed wearily. All five of them, just a little. "How did they know Lark and Lory? Please will someone just tell me . . . I don't know. Everything, I suppose."

"Everything!" Ash sat down next to her and

sighed. "There's a lot to tell, Emily."

"You have to tell me something!" Emily said impatiently. "You can't just stop at, 'Oh, Emily, we're all fairies and you're not, OK?'"

"You ran off and got yourself caught by a load of mad, ancient fairies before we could tell you anything!" Robin snapped. He was still looking furious with Lark and Lory, far more than their parents were.

But Emily was pretty sure he wasn't angry that they'd gone – he minded that they hadn't taken him too.

Eva loosened her arms from Emily a little, so that she could look into her face. "You went through one of the doors into our land, Emily. This house is full of doors to different places. But

171

mostly it's a place where people travel between this world and ours."

Emily nodded slowly. "OK. And why are you here, instead of there?"

"Someone has to watch the doors," Ash explained. "Of course people do come through, sometimes. There's always a bit of coming and going. But we stop the people who shouldn't pass – from either side." Then he grimaced. "Except we weren't watching as well as we should have been. It was stupid of us. . . You've grown up in this house, Emily. You've been here ten years. Even though you're not a fairy, you've absorbed some of the magic that seeps out of the doors. And the doors know you by now."

"Those fairies – they said they'd seen me,"

Emily told him in a gulp. "They said they'd been hoping I'd come."

He nodded grimly. "Fairies like humans, Ems. There's a sort of energy about you. You're so alive. You make us feel more alive too. Those were Ladies of the fairy court. Very, very old. Very powerful."

"Hungry," Eva added quietly.

Ash shivered. "And they know Lark and Lory because we're probably related to most of them. There aren't many of us left, Emily. Fairy children are hardly ever born now. And some of those older fairies would stop at nothing to be a little stronger. Stealing a human child and keeping her as a pet wouldn't worry them at all. You've been so close to them, all this time. Like

173

a rare flower, just out of reach." He sighed. "Of course the doors are easier for you to go through than they would be for any other mortal. We just didn't think. And then tonight, we were all so upset. You were angry. Magic was spitting out all over the place – the door opened without us realizing."

"I'm still angry," Emily said, her voice small. But she wasn't. Not in the same way, not since Lark and Lory had flown her across a fairy land, with hunters chasing after them.

"We didn't want to make you feel as though you were different from Lark and Lory and Robin," Eva said, so quietly that Emily had to lean closer to her to hear. So close that it seemed natural to rest her cheek on her mother's shoulder. She felt

Eva shiver as she touched her, a grateful sort of shudder. Eva's arms tightened round her again.

"I know," Emily murmured back.

"But you are, and we couldn't hide it any longer. We should have found a better way to tell you, but there isn't a good way. That meal – your beautiful cake. We wanted it to be special, somehow. . ."

"You were so tiny," Ash muttered. "This tiny, delicate little thing. I thought it was just an old blanket, you know? But then I heard you laughing."

"Laughing?" Emily stared at him in surprise.

"I know. You were chuckling away to yourself. You were watching the leaves, I think. It was windy, and you were under a willow tree; the branches were moving. And then when I came closer you smiled at me, and you held out your arms, as though you wanted me to pick you up." He was silent for a moment. "So I did."

"There really wasn't anyone else there?" Emily asked quietly. "No one watching?"

Ash shook his head. "No, Emily. I'm sorry."

"Did you make up my birthday?" Emily said, her voice very small. Somehow it seemed important.

"It's the day I found you. We knew it couldn't be your real birthday – we found a nurse to look at you, and she said you were about three months old, at least. But it was the day we wanted to remember." He looked at her worriedly. "Was that wrong?"

"No. . . It would be worse if it was just a day you picked out of nowhere. I think."

"Even though you're upset with us now, I'm still glad I took you," Ash told her fiercely. He was back in his everyday form now, but his eyes sparked and glittered as he stared at her, sharp lights burning deep in the blackness, in a way that definitely wasn't human. "I could feel it as I picked you up, how loving you were, how much you needed someone to love you. And we do, Emily. However different we all are."

"I know you do." Emily swallowed. "Do I have to leave?"

"What?" Eva pulled Emily up to face her. "What do you mean?"

"Now that I know what you are. Does it mean

177

I can't stay here any more?"

"No! No, of course not. We just have to be more careful, that's all. We have to make sure you don't slip through again." She ran her hand lovingly through Emily's black curls. "We should have explained the doors to you years ago, but the time just went past so quickly."

Emily frowned to herself. There was a lot more she wanted to ask, but she was so tired her bones ached. And hungry. Starving, actually. "We never ate the cake," she murmured.

"I did eat a bit of it," Robin admitted. He went red as everyone stared at him. "Only a little bit! When you were taking so long to find out where Emily had gone. It was just sitting there." He glared at them. "Don't look at me like that! I was worried, and it made me feel better. It's a *really* good cake, Ems. Yum."

Emily stood up and hauled her mother up after her. "I bet he had about half of it," she said, almost shyly. "But wouldn't you like some?" She hesitated. "You can really eat it, can't you? You aren't just pretending?"

"I *can* eat it, and I would love some," Eva sighed. "I promise we'll explain everything, Emily. Some things might be hard, but we'll try. But I'm not moving until you understand the most important thing." She threaded her fingers into Emily's hair, around her face. "You belong here. With us. And I promise that you always will."

Emily nodded, trying not to sniff. She knew it was true. Maybe it was a spell, making her so sure, but she didn't care. "Will I ever go back?" she asked, laying one hand over her mother's and glancing hopefully at her father, and Lark and Lory.

Eva looked at Ash, and shrugged, a helpless little twitch of her graceful shoulders. "Ems, I want to say no. I know how dangerous it can be for humans, even though it's also a wonderful place. I want to wrap you in a blanket and tie you to the sofa so you can't go anywhere near any of the doors. . ."

"But you've got a horrible feeling that it won't work." Ash folded his arms. "Never, ever on your own. You have to promise us that, Emily."

"Oh, I do." Emily nodded eagerly. "I'll wait. . ." She turned back, running her fingers gently down Lark and Lory's wings, and shivering delightedly as the warm magic poured through her. She could see it shimmering in the air, like dust motes in sunlight. It tasted sweet – like her own sort of magic.

Emily smiled at her sisters, and then at Robin and Ash and Eva, as she headed for the stairs. "I absolutely need that cake now."

HOLLY has always loved animals. As a child, she had two dogs, a cat, and at one point, nine gerbils (an accident). Holly's other love is books. Holly now lives in Reading with her husband, three sons and a very spoilt cat.

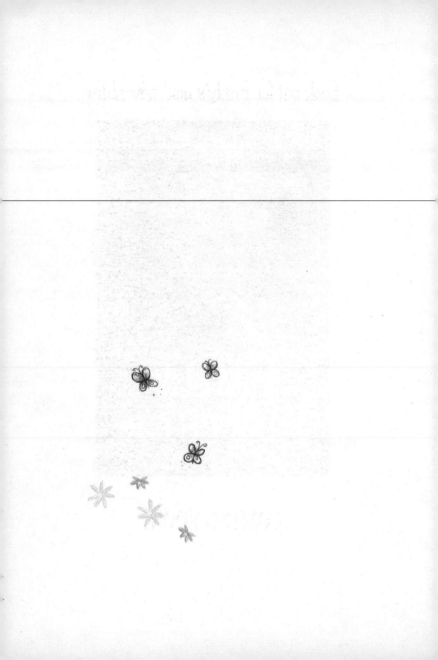

Look out for Emily's next adventure

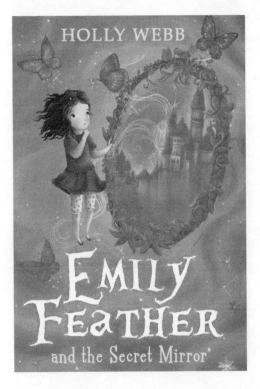

COMING SOON!